232
JERICHO
AVENUE

BY
LEE RICHMOND

This is a work of fiction. Names, characters, businesses, places, events and incidents are either the products of the authors imagination or used in a fictitious manner. Any resemblance to actual person, living or dead, or actual events is purely coincidental.

Copyright 2019 © Lee Richmond

For Marie. Your unwavering love & support made this possible.

A huge thank you to Mark Green for his patience, while proof-reading my work.

I

"May the forces of evil become confused on the way to
your house."

George Carlin

1

The rain was coming down heavily. Its bouncing off the van roof had become almost deafening. Kerry Jones wasn't hearing it though. She was too focused on the comings and goings of number 232 Jericho Avenue.

Kerry and her boyfriend Lester had been sat, staking out this address for the last three hours. It was a typical December night of rainfall and dismal cloud cover and it had grown dark around 16:30 this evening.

For Kerry, wintertime had become more oppressive the older she got. Not that she had ever been a fan. Lester had said that she was suffering from a seasonal affective disorder or SAD as he explained the acronym. Kerry just laughed it off. She always felt sad. The winter just exacerbated things.

The address was rather unremarkable. Sure, it was a nice big property and she could understand how anyone who lived there might only afford to do so if they were well off financially, but as far as townhouses went, this one lacked any semblance of personality which was unusual in houses as old as this was.

"What time are we on now?" Kerry asked, still staring through the rain-washed window.

"It's about 5 minutes since you last inquired," came Lester's irritated response.

Kerry noticed his irritability and ignored it. She wasn't invested in what Lester had to say, anyway. She wasn't even sure why she had bothered to ask. It just seemed like something to say. Something to break the silence. Kerry wasn't fond of the silence. It caused her to spend unwanted time with her thoughts. Her thoughts, of late, were pretty bleak. "Fuck, I hate Christmas!"

"Who hates Christmas?" Lester responded in astonishment.

Again, she disregarded his question. Lester was a nice guy. One of life's happy-go-lucky types. It made perfect sense that he would love this time of year.

"Just imagine if one day you got a phone call." She shifted from the window to give Lester her attention, wanting to establish his response. "The voice at the end of the phone tells you that every single living relative had died in a plane crash."

Lester gave Kerry that bemused smile that someone gives when they don't understand how to respond to something. Try as he might, he couldn't get used to the dark path her thoughts sometimes wandered.

"Erm... Okay?"

"I know that for most people this would be too horrific to even process but imagine how liberating it would be."

"Liberating?"

Kerry could see that what she was saying wasn't sitting well with Lester. This just made her want to continue more. She liked toying with him and making him feel uncomfortable. She supposed it was cruel really, but at least it helped lift her spirits, if only for a short amount of time.

"Yeah," she continued. "Liberating because for the first time in your life you would have nobody to pass judgement on you. Nobody whose standards or expectations you would have to meet."

"You'd still have friends, neighbours, a boss," he added.

"I know, but none of that would matter." She shifted to look back out of the window. "The only people who ever really judge you or expect things from you, who set standards that you can never live up to, are family and if they were suddenly wiped out of your life, well I think once the grief had simmered down, it could be the freest a person could feel."

This all seemed completely ridiculous to Lester. Who in their right mind would value the freedom of losing everyone they ever loved?

"I think you need to see someone," Lester replied. "You need stronger anti-depressants."

He wasn't wrong. She just didn't like to admit it. Sometimes she just said these things to get a reaction, even if she didn't mean what she was saying. As fucked up as she knew it was, dragging Lester down with her somehow helped. Kerry knew this was an unpleasant side to her character yet struggled to care at times like this. Maybe Lester knew what she was doing and didn't want to give her the satisfaction of playing along. She didn't know, and again, didn't care.

"What time is it now?" Kerry asked.

7

"Why do you want to know the time constantly?" Lester snapped.

"This is the third night we have sat here, checking out this address and I'm trying to piece together any routines these people may have."

"Fuck routine." Lester snapped. He was struggling to hide how tired he was growing of continued pestering. He hated it when Kerry went on endlessly about things that he didn't deem important.

"What do you mean, fuck routine?" Kerry asked, becoming annoyed and defensive.

"I mean precisely that. Fuck routine."

"Oh well yeah, fuck routine, fuck having a game plan, let's just blunder in and get caught," Kerry responded sarcastically.

"Okay look," Lester said, shuffling in his seat and placing his hand on Kerry's leg. "These people are old as shit and sitting on a fortune. You've heard the stories right?"

Of course, she had heard how the old couple who lived here were incredibly wealthy. She wouldn't be sat out here if she hadn't. "So?"

"So, we don't need a game plan. They are probably deaf too. It's going to be a simple, good old-fashioned burglary."

Kerry turned towards Lester again and he removed his hand from her leg to brush her long blonde hair away from her eyes. She was naturally a beautiful girl but life, it seemed, had weighed heavily on her over the years, and a smile had become as sparse as the sleep she constantly craved but didn't get much of. He loved her very much, but just sometimes, loving Kerry Jones was hard. She could be so cold and antagonistic.

Sometimes Kerry wished Lester would grow tired of her shit and leave. Not for her sake. More for his. She was convinced he deserved better.

"I don't want to get caught and I don't want anyone to get hurt," Kerry said in a more rational tone.

"I don't want that either," Lester replied. "We get in, we find the dough and we get out. It's that simple."

"And if they catch us? If one of those poor old fuckers should hear us and get up to investigate?"

Lester took his hand from her hair and scratched his beard as if thinking over her question. A gesture that Kerry didn't find particularly encouraging. It was Lester's standard response to being put on the spot when not really having an answer.

"Well, we deal with it."

"Deal with it?" She asked.

"Yeah, but we do it as pleasantly as possible. I mean this couple are especially old. I don't think they have much fight in them, and this reduces the risk of them getting hurt. The threat of being hurt should be enough to keep them in line, so we tie them up and be on our way."

"And what about your brother?" She and Lester's brother Tyler did not get along. In her eyes, he was a violent bully who, when not getting his way, preferred to use his fists as a method for beating his point of view into someone. Tyler and Lester couldn't be any different, and she hated that Lester was so easily manipulated by him.

"What about him?" He asked.

Kerry rolled her eyes. They must have had this discussion a thousand times. "He's a fucking psychopath."

'Here she goes again,' he thought. 'Always over-reacting.' Her use of the word psychopath seemed laughable. "He's not a psychopath. He has a temper. That hardly makes him Jeffrey Dahmer."

"No, he's a psycho. That last job you two pulled, he almost beat that poor bastard half to death."

He couldn't deny that Tyler had gone too far on that occasion, but he found himself trying to add reason behind his actions, anyway. "That guy had a baseball bat. It was him or us."

"So he deserved what Tyler did to him?" Kerry responded, astonished that Lester of all people was going to try to justify what his brother had done to that poor guy. Tyler had messed him up badly. As far as Kerry was concerned, that was not the behaviour of someone in control of his sanity.

"I didn't say that did I?" Lester replied, visibly rattled. "Look," He continued. "I'll control him okay? It's all going to work out fine."

It probably wasn't. Nothing ever really went according to plan, and Lester's denial was becoming harder to accept. Brotherly loyalty was one thing. Ignorance and sheer stupidity was something else entirely.

"Can we just get out of here now?" Kerry asked.

"Okay, sure." Lester turned the key, firing up the engine of the beat-up old Transit van, and pulling away from the kerb.

"I fucking hate Christmas," Kerry muttered to herself.

Had Kerry been looking, she might have noticed a figure behind the curtain of the upstairs window. The silhouette watched as the van disappeared down the avenue before tugging the curtains closed.

II

"We all have a Monster within; the difference is in degree, not in kind."

Douglas Preston - The Monster of Florence

2

"Are you completely fucking mental?" Asked Constable Sean Glasper. He had been on his phone now for forty minutes arguing and it was getting him nowhere. Sean had been on the force for eight years and had always dreamed of being a great cop. His dreams, however, were dashed because his cousin became an especially prolific burglar.

For the last five years, Lester Burrows had been conning Sean into keeping the police off his trail regarding a string of break-ins in the area. The first couple he had done out of a sense of family loyalty, but Lester and his brother Tyler didn't share that sense of loyalty. Every time Sean tried to distance himself from their misdeeds, they resorted to blackmail. Sean had no reason to think Lester would rat him out, but regarding Tyler, anything was possible.

"You know if I go down, I'm taking you with me right?" Came Lester's voice down the phone. "Aiding and abetting doesn't look great on an employment record, and you know how they love Pigs in the slammer."
That same old spiel again, regular as clockwork. Sean knew it word for word.

"Listen, Les, don't try to threaten me. You're not your brother. Save that shit for him, you're better than that." He paused to take a moment to reflect on what he was once again being asked to do. "I can't keep this up much longer. Eventually, I'll get figured out. Either you need to pack it in or leave me out of it."

Lester knew the right strings to pull, and it involved the promise of lots of paper with the Queen's head on them. Sean might have liked to give a speech about how he wanted to do the right thing and take his career seriously, but it was surprising how fast he backtracked when presented with a bundle of cash.

"Okay, Sean here it is. This next job will be worth a fortune. I mean these old bastards are sitting on a Gold Mine."

"And?"

"And I'm telling you, this will be the last time I swear. They don't venture out, they don't use Banks or Building Societies. Everything they have collected throughout their lives sits in that house in jars and tins, scattered here, there and everywhere."

"And you know this how?"

"Tyler has a source. He has it on good authority."

"Oh, Tyler has a source? Well, colour me convinced. Les, why do you swallow every line of bullshit your brother feeds you?"

"Trust me Serpico, and I know you need the money. Just think of the holiday you can take Julie and little Michael on."

Sean took another pause for a moment's contemplation. As compelling a promise as it was, he knew that eventually, the bubble would burst and when that happened; he would regret it for the rest of his life.

"It's Julie and Michael that I'm worried about. If you fuck me it's them that will pay."

"How will we fuck you, Sean?" Lester replied, sounding highly offended by the suggestion. "If we get caught, we take the fall. Nobody will know you had anything to do with it."

As much as Sean would have liked to believe him, that old familiar feeling of self-loathing for being taken as a fool reared its ugly head again. He would regret this, and he knew it.

"Fine. One more time and then that's it. I'm done."

"That's my boy," Lester said through a half chuckle.

"Yeah, fuck you too," Sean said, hanging up the phone.

'When am I going to learn?' He thought to himself. When he had joined the force all those years ago, he never for one second considered that his career could end with him facing jail time.

'Fucking families,' he thought, putting his phone into his pocket.

III

"Nothing is easier than to denounce the evildoer; nothing is more difficult than to understand him."

Fyodor Dostoevsky

3

Kerry had been dipping in and out of sleep for hours. She knew that she should probably try to stay up as even a half an hour cat nap would guarantee her a night of tossing and turning come bedtime. Every time she slipped into subconsciousness, it was the same old dream that snapped her back out of it. This dream, however, came with no visuals, only an audio soundtrack.

It's dark. Not the darkness that people usually experience when they stumble to the bathroom in the middle of the night and stub their toe on the couch. This darkness is oppressive. She is wearing it like a thick, suffocating blanket over the head. Kerry's eyes won't adjust to a point where they become useful, but her other senses are working overtime.

That smell. The smell of decay. So overpowering that she chokes on it. So pungent that she can taste it. It's unlikely that anybody could explain what death tastes like, but at this moment, Kerry could. It tasted like what she imagined old cabbage that had been soaked in battery acid would taste like. It made her want to retch.

Worse still is the screaming. Shrill and shrieking and coming from all directions. Even in the realm of dreams, Kerry can feel the fine hairs on her skin stand on end as if they were being excited by static. Every time, it becomes so overwhelming that Kerry falls to her knees with her arms clamped tightly around her head to shield her from whatever looms in the vast absence of light, as if being enveloped in her own arms will somehow protect her, and every time she jolts awake covered in sweat.

Kerry stood at the sink, her face dripping with the cold water she had splashed on herself in a vague attempt to feel more human.

"What the fuck is wrong with me?" she rhetorically asked her reflection in the bathroom cabinet.

Grabbing a towel from the radiator, Kerry headed into the bedroom. She dried her face and hair and threw the towel onto her bed before changing into her clothes. Kerry only ever wore black these days. Lester often joked that she was the female reincarnation of Johnny Cash. Tyler, always the less pleasant of the two, just referred to her as that moody, Goth bitch. Not that Kerry cared.

She headed down the stairs two steps at a time and grabbed her leather jacket off the hook before leaving the house and jumping into her crappy old Nissan. She was already running behind after having succumbed to her traumatic attempt at a nap.

Kerry fired up the engine and with her tyres squealing, gunned it down the road fully aware that she would take some flak for not being there at the agreed time. Tyler was an absolute dick about things like that and when it came to Kerry, like a Dog with a bone.

'Fucking dick.' She thought as she sped towards the Burger King, where they had agreed to meet.

She constantly questioned why Lester found it necessary to involve his brother in these jobs. The psycho had a loose wire and every time he tagged along things got messy. She could still see the face of the last guy they raided. Tyler had beaten him to an unrecognisable pulp. He had survived the battering. Kerry had monitored that outcome, but it permanently changed his life after the assault, and she doubted it was just his physical well-being that would have suffered. It would surely screw with his state of mind too. What makes it worse is that they came away with pocket change. Lester and Tyler had brought the job to her on the promise that their victim was minted, but after the burglary, they found themselves in possession of about £320 plus a Blu-Ray player that Tyler had swiped as they were leaving. If Tyler's "source" had been so wrong about that, then why is he being trusted now?
Kerry had done trying to protest over Tyler's involvement. Lester wasn't interested in her opinion of his brother, and she knew it. Still, this was to be her last job, and she figured that if they could just get in and get what they came for with no major problem, she wouldn't have to see him anymore. It's not like he popped round for coffee and a natter. She wasn't going to pretend she liked him.

IV

"It is very hard for evil to take hold of the unconsenting soul."

Ursula K. Le Guin - A Wizard of Earthsea

4

The Burger King where they had agreed to meet was located in a retail park just outside of Cackle Hill town centre. Kerry turned into the car park at high speed. She was already running thirty-five minutes late and the icy roads hadn't helped her journey one bit. Tyler would never let her off for her tardiness. It would be one of those days. She just hoped she had the strength to get through it without telling them all to go fuck themselves.

'Just focus on the bigger picture,' she thought, trying to convince herself that it would be worth all the attitude she had to fend off.

"Well, hallelujah," Tyler said, in a loud but not so loud as to be shouting voice. "What time did we say?"

"Okay, don't be an arsehole," Kerry replied, pulling up a chair next to Lester.

Lester put his hand on Kerry's leg and pecked her on the cheek. "You okay, honey?" He asked with genuine concern. He always knew when she was having 'an off day' as he called them. Today was definitely one of those days. He only had to look at her to know this.

Public displays of affection turned her stomach and Lester knew this. She was sure he did it just to annoy her. She didn't do public kissing, and she wasn't inclined to walk through the street holding hands either.

"No, I had a rough night, and then I dozed off this morning and.."

"The nightmares again?" He asked.

'Why does he continue to ask me questions to which he already knows the answer?' Kerry thought. "I don't want to talk about it now. You want to go grab me a coffee, babe?"

"Sure," Lester replied, climbing out of his seat. "You want anything to eat?"

"No, I'm good thanks, just coffee is fine."

Kerry watched as Lester headed over to the counter to get her drink. She didn't need eyes in the back of her head to know that Tyler was still glaring in her direction. She could feel his stare burning into the back of her skull. "I can feel your look," she said through gritted teeth.

"Oh really? Well, it's nice to know you've shown up nice and alert." He said in a mock tone. "Late as fuck, but alert none the less."

"Oh, kiss my arse." She snapped back.

"Yeah, I'll take a pass on that if it's all the same to you."

Lester reappeared with her coffee and set himself back at the table. He passed the coffee to Kerry and then took hold of her hand. Her hands were freezing as the heater in her car had given up working last winter so she had driven to meet them in an icebox.

"So do we have a plan of action?" Kerry asked.

"We do," Tyler replied. "We've just got to hold on for a few more minutes as this isn't all of us."

Confused glances were thrown in Tyler's direction. Kerry waited a moment, but Lester would not chirp up so once again, she had to play the mouthpiece to his silent partner. "Wait, you're bringing more people in?"

Tyler nodded and began to answer with a mouthful of bacon sandwich. "That's right. We'll need more hands-on-deck to help carry the dough and make sure that shit doesn't get out of hand."

Kerry couldn't believe what she was hearing. She turned to Lester, who still sat silently with a dumbstruck expression on his face. "So, you're okay with this?"

Lester turned to Kerry with the look of someone who had been caught with his trousers around his ankles. He was now truly between a rock and a hard place and no answer that he could give would be the right one. The coward in him took hold as he decided that Tyler's bite was worse than hers. "I know what you're going to say but Tyler's right…"

"Un-fucking-believable," Kerry protested. "I could have bet money on you taking his side."

"Look, we can't afford any fuck-ups on this job and if we need a few extra bodies, then so be it."

Kerry could feel her blood starting to boil. She loved Lester but, if there was one thing that pissed her off; it was how he foolishly went along with everything his big brother suggested. It was only a matter of time before his idolisation of Tyler got him either jailed or deceased.

Kerry tried to keep her cool. Losing it at this point would be futile and it was far too busy in the restaurant to be making a scene. "Right, has it ever occurred to either of you that the reason they have never caught us is that we keep things small and simple?"

"Hey Lester, isn't that what you're calling your sex book?"

"Fuck you, man," Lester replied, extending his middle finger towards Tyler.

"It's okay, I can wait for you both to grow up." Kerry interrupted, still trying to keep her temper in check.

Tyler was just about to respond with some sarcastic jibe when the door to the restaurant disturbed his train of thought. He turned to see who had entered and on recognising them, beckoned them over. Kerry had never seen either of them before, which made her even more uneasy. The first of the two was a tall, Raven-haired girl, who Kerry would have placed around twenty-four-ish, give or take a year. She was pretty but sported far too much in the way of facial piercings for Kerry's liking.

The second of the two was maybe a year or two older than the first. He was a big-built guy and even under his winter coat, Kerry could tell he was well put together.

The new arrivals joined them at the table and Tyler set about introducing everybody. "This is Shane and his lovely lady friend Teri. They will be joining us. You have already heard me talking about Lester, my brother and his girlfriend, Kerry."

"What, no lovely Kerry?" Kerry interjected.

Teri leaned over to shake Kerry's hand to which she responded, unenthusiastically. Teri took the hint and sat back down.

Tyler leaned onto the table to address everyone all at once. "There has been a slight change of plans."

"What do you mean?" Kerry asked.

He cracked a smile that always broke across his face when he knew he was about to upset Kerry. "We're moving things forward."

"How forward?" She inquired again.

"Tomorrow night."

"Are you fucking kidding me?" Kerry responded, oblivious that she had raised her voice enough to turn a few heads. "We had this all planned out for next week so why are you changing it now?"

Tyler leaned in towards Kerry. He had that look in his eye she had seen many times before. Usually around the time that he became frighteningly unstable. "What does it matter?" he said. "We can sit on this another week or we can get it over and done with tomorrow night."

Looking around the room, it appeared that she was the only one who had a problem with this. "It matters because we planned it that way and we don't change plans."

Lester had decided that he had best become involved in the dispute before things turned ugly. Tyler had a significant mean streak in him, but Kerry would never let that back her down. Besides, he didn't like how much attention the two were now attracting due to their flaring tempers. "Kerry, it doesn't matter. We know what we're meant to be doing and, to be honest, there isn't that much to plan." He put his hand on her arm as if expecting that the gesture would somehow calm her down. She pushed it away and threw him a look that suggested he should drop dead on the coffee shop floor.

"He's right," Tyler weighed in. "We go in and we split up and start searching the house for the money. It's hidden all over the place. The old fuckers should be sound asleep by then and, from what I understand, they're both stone deaf anyway. We clean them out and we leave. It's not that complicated."

Shane spoke up for the first time since arriving. "This'll be a piece of cake. I've done this a thousand times."

"Thanks for the input new guy," Kerry snapped. "How about you let us worry about what we are doing and how easy it will or won't be?"

Shane laughed off her comment. "I see what you mean Ty. This bitch is well aggressive."

"What the fuck did you just call me?" Kerry said, trying to stand up out of her seat. Lester caught her arm and was trying to make her sit back down. Teri found the whole thing highly entertaining and started to laugh, which did nothing to pacify the situation.

"Okay, for fuck's sake shut up all of you." This time it was Lester who was raising his voice. He was usually such a calm, calculated character and Kerry still wasn't used to those rare occasions when his cool demeanour would slip. "Tomorrow night we are bagging what should be a life-changing haul. We should be loaded and won't have to keep pulling this shit, so can we please just hold it together for another couple of days?"

Kerry sat down like a reprimanded child and picked up her coffee. "Fine," she replied, scowling into her mug.

"Tyler?" Lester demanded.

"Fine, whatever."

"Great," Lester said. "So tomorrow night, we meet on the east side of the town park at 22:30. Everyone clear on that?"

They all nodded in understanding and started to gather their things.

"Get a good night's sleep ladies and gentlemen," Tyler added. "Tomorrow will be a long, busy night."

V

"It is as inhuman to be totally good as it is to be totally evil."

Anthony Burgess - A Clockwork Orange

5

The Television was the only thing illuminating the otherwise dark bedroom. David Cronenberg's The Fly was playing and Jeff Goldblum was demonstrating his newfound ability to climb walls, but nobody was watching it. Kerry had been laying there for fifteen minutes, going through the motions and making all the right noises in all the right places, just hoping that Lester would hurry and finish writhing around on top of her.

Sex had never been something that Kerry had craved much. She gave in to it because Lester seemed to enjoy it and wasn't that what couples did? The truth of the matter was that she just wasn't an overtly, intimate person and with so much weighing on her lately, coupled with the lack of sleep, she, more than ever, was not in the mood.

Lester hadn't noticed, however, and was busy enjoying himself, regardless.

Lester inevitably started making those familiar grunting noises that Kerry took as a sign that he was all done and sure enough, Lester rolled off of her and reached for his pack of smokes. He popped a cigarette into his mouth, lit it and then laid down on his pillow and balanced an ashtray on to his still heaving chest.

"You feeling more relaxed now?" He asked.

"Sure," Kerry replied, half-heartedly.

"Wow. Way to make a guy feel special."

Kerry turned towards him and started to stroke his arm. "I'm sorry. I'm just a little freaked out about tomorrow night."

"Why?" Lester asked, a little too snappy for Kerry's liking.

"You know why," Kerry answered. She stopped stroking his arm and turned to face away.

"I know you're unhappy with the changes to the plans. I'm not thrilled either but it is what it is."

"You could stand up to Tyler once in a while, you know."

Lester rolled his eyes and stubbed his cigarette out.

"In fact, you could stand up for me once in a while, too." She added.

"Well, you have a habit of winding him up sometimes Kerry. Maybe if you didn't provoke him so much."

"Seriously?" she replied, more than a little pissed off.

Lester knew he had rubbed her up the wrong way now, but he had a point to make. Lester had a severe problem with choosing to make a point over, taking the easy life. "I know you two don't get along and, I'm not suggesting that you should try, but, Tyler has a bad temper and ever since we were kids growing up, I have never seen him back down from anyone."

"So you're saying that I need to be the one that backs down?"

"That's not what I mean." Lester cradled his head in exasperation. "Why can't we just be one of those couples that cuddle after sex?"

Kerry found his question to be funny enough that a laugh escaped her mouth and instantly she knew that Lester was not impressed. "Because we're not one of those couples and never have been."

"Okay fine," Lester said, turning his back on Kerry. "We had better get some sleep. It'll be a long night tomorrow."

"Fine, Goodnight," Kerry replied, staring blankly towards the wall.

"I love you," Lester said as he closed his eyes, hoping that sleep would find him soon. Kerry ignored it.

VI

"What would your good do if evil didn't exist, and what would the earth look like if all the shadows disappeared?"

Mikhail Bulgakov

6

Kerry found herself in the dark once again. The familiar stink of death and decay had worked its way deep into her nostrils. It was a smell she never got used to. It made her feel sick to her stomach.

The Screaming seemed louder than ever before now, violating her ears and exploding into her brain like the worst migraine she had ever experienced.

It all seemed different this time. She felt eyes on her. She couldn't see them, she just knew they were there. Watching her. How? She had no idea. If she couldn't see her hand in front of her face, how the hell were they able to see her?

Suddenly, a hand thrust out of the blackness and seized the back of her neck and...

...Kerry bolted upright in her bed. She was shaking and the sweat that was running off her face had visibly soaked her pillow. Her t-shirt clung tightly to her body, heavy and darkened with perspiration. "What the fuck?" She muttered quietly to herself.

The dream had been a constant for a good while now but, had never really changed. It had always woken Kerry with a powerful feeling of terror, but this was the first time that anything within the dream had grabbed her. She almost felt as though the hand still had a grip on the back of her neck. Instinctively she swatted at it, but there was nothing there.

Kerry took a moment to get her bearings. She could hear the shower running in the en-suite bathroom. She leaned over to Lester's bedside table and removed one of his cigarettes from the packet. Lighting it, she inhaled deeply. The nicotine-laced smoke felt welcome as it entered her lungs.

"How did you sleep?" Lester asked, entering the bedroom with a towel wrapped around his waist.
"You know, the usual."
He examined her pale, sweat-drenched face. "You look like shit." He replied.
Kerry stuck her middle finger up at him. "Thanks."
"Want some breakfast?" He asked, snickering at her gesture. "I'm doing some scrambled egg."
"Just some coffee, please."
He shook his head. "You should eat."
"You should mind your own fucking business." She retorted.
"Sorry I spoke." Lester stormed out of the bedroom, annoyed.
"Why am I such an arsehole?" She muttered out of earshot to Lester.

Kerry extinguished her cigarette and went into the bathroom to shower. She felt grim because of the unenthusiastic sex and the nightmare sweats. She thumbed through her phone playlist looking for music that would suit her mood as she showered and decided on Slayers 'Reign in Blood' album. "Perfect." She said, hitting play and switching the shower on.

The news was full of tributes to some actor who had been discovered dead in a hotel bathtub, from what appeared to be a drug overdose. Kerry had never heard of this actor. Apparently, he had been big in the '80s but she didn't care too much. Kerry was more interested in her third cup of coffee and what must be her seventh cigarette. She wasn't counting.

It seemed pointless to keep telling Lester how she had a terrible feeling about tonight. He wasn't concerned. He placed far too much faith in Tyler and Kerry worried that misplaced faith would be their ruin. Besides who were these newbies? Friends of Tyler's? That did nothing to appease her apprehensions.

"You're smoking all my cigarettes." Lester protested.
"Huh?" Kerry replied obliviously.
"Hey welcome back. What was it like where you were?"
"Sorry, I'm just fucking tired, and all those Christmas lights you insisted on putting up have given me a headache."
"Well, why don't you stop throwing the coffee back and go get forty winks?" Lester suggested.
Kerry thought back to the dream that had wakened her in a state of dread and panic this morning. "Nah fuck that. I'm okay. I just need some air this morning."

"Okay, but be careful in case all that caffeine gives you the jitters. We need you in fine fettle this evening."

"It isn't my first rodeo," Kerry replied, more than a little offended.

"It's the first one where the score has been this big though and that's why we can't afford any fuck-ups."

Kerry ignored the words coming out of Lester's mouth. "Can I have another fag?"

"Yeah, but this is my last one," he protested.

"I will go out and buy you more. Quit bitching and give me the cigarette."

Lester removed the smoke from the packet and threw it at Kerry. "You're a pain in my arse."

Kerry gave Lester the finger for the second time that morning.

VII

"Demons are like obedient dogs; they come when they are called."

Remy de Gourmont

7

Lester's transit van pulled on to the Cackle Hill ring road. It was extraordinary for Lester to be so openly furious with his brother, but on this occasion; he felt justified. Lester had arrived at Tyler's house at 2 pm as instructed so they could load up his equipment, ready for tonight only to discover that Tyler wasn't home. Upon further investigation, he soon located Tyler in his local Pub. If that wasn't bad enough, by the time he had dragged Tyler out of the Pub he was already half-drunk.

"Are you fucking stupid?" Lester yelled over the top of the Van stereo that Tyler had defiantly switched on to drown Lester's indignant protest.

"It was a few drinks, that's all." Tyler reasoned while struggling not to laugh. This only wound Lester up more.

"You like to give it the big man around town. You act like you're fucking Scarface or something when in reality, we are common crooks, yet when we finally have a job worth pulling off you put the whole thing in jeopardy by getting pissed with your mates."

"Now you're being ridiculous," Tyler countered.

"Ridiculous?" Lester snapped. "I fight your corner every single day. All I hear is how Tyler's a two-bit thug. Tyler's a drunken yob. Tyler's an irresponsible arsehole."

"Let me guess, Kerry, right?" He asked, laughing.

"No, it's not just Kerry. Believe it or not, there is a list as long as my arm of people who think badly of you and I spend my entire life sticking up for you." Lester reached down and switched the stereo off. "Keep that shit off when I'm talking to you."

Tyler turned to Lester with a grin on his face. "Look, little bro, I'm sorry. What do you want me to say?"

"You could start by admitting that you're a dick."

"Fine, if it makes you happy, I'm a dick."

"Right well, we need to get you some coffee. In case it escaped your notice, we have a big job to pull and if Kerry gets wind that you have been out on the piss, I'll never hear the end."

"Man, fuck that Bitch!"

Lester pulled the Van into a layby and slammed the brakes on, hard, forcing Tyler to lurch forward and hit his knees on the dashboard.

"What the fuck?" He shouted, grabbing his now sore legs.

Lester spun towards Tyler, pushing his index finger towards his brother's face. "Okay, listen up because I'm getting sick and tired of saying it. Kerry is my girl, and I'm sick of this shit between the two of you."

"Okay man, calm down."

"No, I will not calm down. You can't keep talking about her that way."

Tyler pushed Lester's finger aside. "First, don't fucking point at me. Second, I don't for a second believe that she doesn't sit around bad-mouthing me."

"Does it not occur to you that she wouldn't feel that way towards you if you didn't behave like a prick?"

Tyler put his head into his hands and began rubbing the sides of his skull as if to physically communicate his frustration. "She doesn't have to like me, Les."

"No, I know but, if we are going to have to work together, it would make it a fuck of a lot simpler if I wasn't constantly torn between the two of you."

Tyler lifted his head and looked at Lester. He, once again, wore that stupid grin that Lester hated. "I promise to be nicer, but you have to tell her to get off my back."

"Okay, deal." Lester agreed. He started up the ignition and drew the van back on to the ring road. "Let's get you some coffee."

"So what's her deal, anyway?" Tyler asked.

"What?" Lester replied, clueless as to what he was being asked.

"Kerry. What's her deal?"

"What do you mean, what's her deal?" Lester asked, none the wiser.

Tyler took a smoke from the packet in his shirt pocket, put it into his mouth, and lit the end. "Don't tell me you haven't noticed how uptight she is?"

Lester motioned to Tyler to give him a cigarette. Tyler obliged and held out his lighter to spark it for him. "She isn't uptight," Lester replied, having removed the cigarette from his mouth.

"No shit?" came Tyler's reply.

"She has just had a tough time of it that's all."

"Haven't we all?" Tyler replied, a little too unsympathetically for Lester's liking.

"No, not like Kerry, we haven't."

"What makes her shit so much worse then?"

Lester took another drag on his smoke. "She doesn't like to have it talked about." He answered.

"I won't say shit, I promise," Tyler replied, crossing his fingers and holding them up for Lester to see.

"You can't say I told you okay?"

"I mean it mate. Cross my heart," he promised. Even going as far as to act out the motion of actually crossing his heart.

"Okay." Lester took a deep puff on his cigarette before throwing the butt out of the window. "When she was just a little kid, her father raped her older sister."

"Holy shit!" Tyler gasped. "That's fucking rough."

"It doesn't end there. They took Kerry and her sister into care. Turns out their mother knew and did nothing about it." Lester unscrewed the cap on a bottle of water he had in the cup holder and took a swig before setting it down and replacing the cap. "They had been living with this Foster family for about three years when one morning, Kerry got up and went into the bathroom to find her sister dead in the tub. She had slashed her wrists."

"Okay, I give you that. It's a shit-show of a time." Tyler lit another cigarette and offered one to Lester, who shook his head. "So did the parents go down for it then?"

"The father did. Her mother got off as there was no real evidence to support a conviction."

"Then what happened?" Tyler asked.

"Kerry's old man got about a year into his sentence before he tied one end of his bedsheet around his bunk and the other around his neck."

Tyler shook his head in disbelief. "The bastard took the easy way out then?"

"Yeah, you could say that," Lester replied. "Probably grew tired of the constant beatings that get dished out to the nonce's."

"What about her mum?"

"Kerry doesn't know where her mother is. She hasn't seen her since."

"Fuckin Hell."

"You can't say anything," Lester repeated.

"I won't say shit Les, you have my word."

"So maybe now you can see why she is a bit tightly wound?"

Tyler nodded. "Yeah, it makes sense I suppose."

The Van pulled off the main road and into the car park of a Starbucks.

"Coffee," Lester said.

"Lots." Tyler agreed.

VIII

"And what constitutes evil, real evil, is the taking of a single human life. Whether a man would die tomorrow or the day after or eventually... it doesn't matter. Because if God does not exist, then life... every second of it... Is all we have."

Anne Rice - Interview with the Vampire

8

Kerry had been pacing the living room for what seemed like hours when the van pulled in to the driveway. As Lester and Tyler exited the van, Kerry was already at the door to meet them.

"Where the fuck have you two been?" She asked.

Lester came over to hug her. "We got delayed a little."

"Yeah, it's my fault," Tyler interjected. "I couldn't find all of my rucksacks. Sorry."

Kerry had never once heard Tyler apologise to her in all the years she had known him. It effectively took the wind out of her sails.

"It's fine." She said, a little deflated. "You're here now."

They entered the house and walked through to the breakfast bar in the kitchen. Tyler and Lester took a seat and Kerry walked over to the kettle.

"Coffee?" she asked.

Lester and Tyler both exchanged a smile. "No, I'm good thanks," Lester replied.

"I'm good too, thanks," Tyler added.

Kerry filled the kettle and switched it on. "So where are we at then?"

Tyler took a piece of paper from his trouser pocket and opened it to reveal a checklist. "The van is tooled up so I can check that off."

"Do we need the baseball bats?" Kerry asked. "This is an old couple, not a pair of Green Beret's."

"It's purely for show, should they wake and discover us. We wave them around. I guarantee you they won't say or do shit."

"I hope you're right," Kerry said with a look of apprehension on her face. "We can't have a repeat of last time."

"We won't," Tyler said as reassuringly as he could muster. "No old fool will rush someone with a bat in their hand. That kind of stupidity is reserved for the younger hotheads with something to prove."

Lester decided that he had better chirp up, wishing to have some influence over Tyler's actions. "Do whatever you need to do to get them to back down Ty, but don't hurt them okay?"

"I'll be on my best behaviour." He laughed.

"I'm serious man. I'm not leaving the scene with someone's grandparents laying there injured, or worse."

"Trust me," Tyler replied.

Lester nodded. "Okay fair enough." He turned to Kerry and clapped his hands together. "Right I'm starving and we need to eat before we leave. Who wants pizza?"

"If you're buying," Tyler answered.

Kerry shook her head in reply. The last thing she needed was a belly full of greasy food. She felt nauseous enough as it was, and Stan and Ollie were not helping to ease her tension.

Tonight was a disaster waiting to happen and all the pizza and reassurance in the world would not convince her otherwise.

"You need to eat something, babe."

"I will have a sandwich or something later. I'm far too nervous to eat pizza." She stirred her coffee and then joined the other two sitting at the breakfast bar. "Are you sure we can trust the others?" She enquired.

Tyler responded, a little too hastily and defensively. "I've known Shane for years."

"What about the girlfriend?" Lester added.

"Well, admittedly, not that long but Shane vouched for her and I trust him."

"Okay good enough," Lester said.

"Erm... Not really," Kerry replied. She loathed it when Lester spoke for her. She didn't share his opinion and he should have known better.

"It's too late now, Kerry," Tyler countered. "They are in it up to their neck and you don't drop team members once they are up to speed with the plan."

Kerry took a sip of her coffee. It was far too hot to drink, and she winced as it burnt her tongue. 'Great,' she thought. 'Maybe it's an omen.' "I still think you should have consulted with us before taking it upon yourself to recruit outsiders."

Ever the voice of diplomacy, Lester decided to end the debate before the usual bickering started. "You may be right Kerry, but what's done is done. Let's just do this as smoothly as possible and all being well, when we wake up tomorrow we will be minted."

Kerry finished her coffee and got up to leave the room. "Fine." She said as she walked out.

Lester looked over to Tyler, who was sitting, scowling in her direction and shrugged his shoulders. 'I give up,' he thought.

IX

"All evil is good become cancerous."

Isaac Asimov

9

The Christmas lights that decorated the houses along Park Road shimmered through the torrential rain that fell from the sky, creating a small stream along the kerbside. As the van turned the corner, its wheels produced a mini tsunami in the gutter. Two figures stood shivering on the side of the road, their dark blue raincoats doing little to prevent them from being soaked by the downpour.

The van slowed and drew up to the kerb in front of them, and Tyler slid the side door open, beckoning them in.

"Get your arse's in quick before you catch pneumonia."

Shane and Teri jumped into the van and began taking their macs off as Tyler shut the door behind them.

"Holy shit that's some rain. Anyone have a towel?" Shane asked.

Tyler plucked up an old hand towel that Lester had been using for van repairs and oil checks. "Best I can do you I'm afraid."

Shane regarded the towel for a second and then shrugged and began using it to dry his hair. "Fuck it." He said.

"You're late," Teri said, in a tone that implied she was more than a little vexed.

Kerry turned from the front seat, fixing Teri with an icy stare. "There was an accident on the ring road. We haven't yet mastered control of the weather, or peoples shitty driving." She had already figured out that she and Teri would not make good friends.

"Okay sorry I spoke," Teri replied, raising her hands in submission.

Kerry turned back in her seat and looked out at the rain drenching the windscreen. The window wipers were passing back and forth at full speed but couldn't clear it fast enough. "Jesus, can you even see anything?" she asked.

Lester was in full concentration mode, leaning forward in his seat to get a better view ahead. "Nope, not so much."

"Maybe you better slow down a little then." She suggested. "Better to get there a little late and not be dead."

"You think?" came Lester's sardonic reply.

Tyler leaned over the back of Kerry's seat to get a view of the road ahead. "She has a point, Les. Let's not die tonight."

Lester motioned to his brother to back off. If there was one thing he hated, it was people telling him how to drive. Lester was an amiable bloke but something happened to him when he climbed behind the wheel of a vehicle. All his finer qualities drowned in a sea of anger and hatred. If he ever got arrested for murder, it would be because someone pushed him that bit too far while he was driving. "Don't tell me how to drive" he snapped.

"I'm not telling you how to fucking drive. I'm requesting you don't kill us." He sat back down. "All that money will be useless if we die before we can spend it."

"We're five minutes away. I'm positive I can keep you alive for five minutes."

"You people always this argumentative before a job?" Teri joked.

Shane started to laugh. "Maybe we need to keep them from killing each other, let alone the people we're robbing."

The transit pulled into Jericho Avenue and drove on towards the end where there was a small green on the left-hand side.

"Pull up just here," Tyler said. "We don't want to park right outside. It looks too suspicious."

Lester applied the brakes, and the van came to a standstill.

"What time is it Les?" asked Tyler.

Lester checked his watch. "22:50." He replied.

"Okay great," Tyler said, reaching for the black bin bag by his side. "We don't go in until 23:00." He rummaged through his bag and began passing out rucksacks. "Each of you takes one of these and when we get in, you fill them with as much cash and valuables as you can find."

"What's the time frame?" Shane asked, taking a rucksack.

"I don't want us in there any longer than half an hour. We keep quiet, but we move fast. Check tins, jars, drawers or anywhere else you can think of."

"No problem," Shane replied.

Tyler reached back into the bag and pulled out a handful of balaclava's and passed them around. "Keep these on at all times, because should the inhabitants wake up we don't want them seeing our faces."

"Is the place alarmed?" Shane asked.

"Kerry will go in first and take care of the alarm. Once she has done her thing we can go in."

"Sweet."

Lester took hold of Kerry's hand. "You ready, honey?"

Kerry squeezed his hand and then pulled her balaclava down over her face. "Oh, yes." She answered.

X

"There's only one great evil in the world today. Despair."

Evelyn Waugh - Vile Bodies

10

Kerry had taken longer than she had expected gaining access into the house. The door had seemed impossible to infiltrate. She had eventually found more luck with a window around the side, which she had entered by cutting a section of the glass so she could flip the latch and slide it open. The only problem was that she was further from the alarm panel then she would have liked.

Gracefully, she slipped inside and raced, as quietly as she could to the alarm board. Once there she used a screwdriver to pop the panel open.

Locating the power supply, she quickly unplugged it and then shot back over to the board. Knowing she had mere seconds before the alarm sounded, she scanned the panel for the backup battery. No sooner had she discovered it than she unplugged it. Pulling the wire from the battery, the system powered down, and the alarm remained silent. Kerry let out a sigh of relief before heading to the front door.

"Paranoid much?" She whispered to herself, studying the door. The entire lock side of the door was covered in deadbolts. The only way she could have gotten in would have been with a battering ram. One by one, she began pulling bolts until they were all unlocked. The door was on a Yale lock so she popped the handle and opened it up.

"There she is" Tyler pointed towards the figure emerging from the doorway. "Okay, masks on. Let's go."

They all quietly departed the van and headed, quickly, over to the house.

"Quick, hurry," Kerry whispered, inviting them in.

Tyler was the last one through and Kerry gently closed the door behind him.

"Okay, use only your torchlight. No turning the lights on." Tyler whispered, just loud enough that they all could hear. "Lester, you and I will head upstairs, you three can cover down here."

Kerry nodded. "Be careful and don't fuck up."

Tyler let out a quiet laugh. "We'll be fine. Search every room. You have half an hour, max, but be thorough."

"What if we clean them out before then?" Shane asked, a little louder than necessary.

"Shh, for fuck's sake keep it down." Kerry softly scolded him.

"If you have checked everywhere and we are not finished, keep hunting until we are," Tyler instructed. "Nobody is finished until I say we are finished."

"Okay come on, we're wasting time," Lester added. He turned to Kerry and put his hand on her arm. "Good luck."

They all headed in separate directions, ready to ransack the house.

XI

"You or I might think that at least one would show courage and put up a fight. But neither you nor I have suffered as they, and even we have born witness in silence to lesser ills under less dire threat. Yet, in the face of evil, to sit silent is an even greater evil. Complacency is ever the enabler of darkest deeds;"

Robert Fanney

11

Kerry had been going through the kitchen cupboards for about ten minutes. She had opened every container. Searched every jar and pan, yet had turned up nothing. Her backpack, so far, remained barren.

Shane was busying himself in the pantry, also to no avail.

"Hey, Blondie," he whispered over to Kerry.

"What?" she answered with a scowl.

"You found anything yet?"

She hadn't, and it was starting to worry her. "No, fuck all."

Shane was swiftly growing impatient and as a result, had begun slamming things around with little regard for the fact that he could be waking up the residents.

"Please be quiet," Kerry said in a hushed yet angry tone. "Are you trying to get us busted?"

"There's nothing here." He pulled another jar from a shelf. Inspected it and then put it aside. "We're totally screwed."

Kerry closed the cupboard door and walked over to the pantry.

"Look, don't freak out. Maybe Lester and Tyler are having better luck upstairs."

Teri appeared, having been going through the dining-room, next door. "Any luck?"

Shane threw her an anguished look. "Not a fucking bean."

"The dining rooms a bust too," she replied. "Everything's empty. It's fucking weird."

"Are you fucking kidding me?" Shane said through clenched teeth, turning around and walking up to Kerry aggressively. "You promised us Fort Knox and we've got fuck all."

"Firstly, back the fuck up," Kerry threatened, squaring up to Shane as he advanced. "Calm down and don't try to intimidate me, because I'm not impressed. There has to be something of value down here." "Well, there isn't in there," Teri added.

Shane turned to Teri with a desperate look on his face. "There has to be something. Silverware or electrical goods. Anything."

"Not a thing," Teri answered. "Every single cupboard and drawer is empty."

"It's the same here," Kerry said. "Other than the odd frying pan or scrubbing brush, there is nothing."

"All I have here is a selection of empty jars and tubs. There isn't even any food."

"What?" Kerry asked, doubtfully. "There has to be food."

Shane could feel his temper begin to get the better of him. "I just fucking said, there is no food. No food, no money, no heirlooms, fuck all."

Kerry opened the cupboard situated under the sink and began rooting through its sparse contents. "God, I hope they find something upstairs."

Upstairs, however, things weren't much better. Lester had pulled the small bedroom at the end of the landing to pieces, exploring as frantically yet quietly as he could. He had searched under the bed, through the drawers, in the wardrobe. His search had turned up nothing.

Tyler appeared behind him and whispered into his ear, "Found anything yet?"

Lester, who hadn't heard him come in, felt his heart leap into his throat. "Jesus Christ Tyler, don't creep up like that."

Tyler would have found this amusing, were it not for the fact that he was so pissed off. "I've been through that bathroom and nothing. Through that other empty bedroom and nothing."

"There's nothing in here either. You think they found anything downstairs?"

Before Tyler could answer, they saw Kerry appear at the top of the stairs. Quietly, she made her way to the room, where both men stood.

"Any joy?" Tyler demanded, visibly wound up.

"No, there is nothing down there. It's fucking bizarre. It's like they own nothing. How about you guys?"

"Same here," Lester added.

"I can't fucking believe this," Tyler said, in an audible outburst that was sure to get them caught.

"Jesus," Kerry sighed. "Keep it down or they'll hear you."

Tyler composed himself and commenced whispering again. "You know what this means, don't you?"

"What?" Kerry asked.

"It means, in all probability, that they keep all the money in where they sleep."

"Okay, maybe. So, what, we come back when they have gone out?"

"No Kerry, for all we know, they never go out. Old people are weird like that."

"You can't mean that you propose to go into their room while they're sleeping?"

"That's precisely what I mean."

Kerry threw a disturbed glance at Lester, who had much the same expression on his face. "Come on Tyler, " Lester urged. "Just forget it."

Tyler let out a stifled laugh. "Relax. They won't even know I'm there."

Lester seized hold of Tyler's arm, forcibly swinging him around so they were facing. "We should rethink this."

"Quit being such a cunt Les," Tyler said, yanking his arm free of Lester's grip. "I will be in and out. The deaf old bastards won't even know I'm there."

With that, Tyler walked out of the room and smoothly opened the door to the main bedroom. He looked at Lester and Kerry, flashing them one last smug grin before sliding through the doorway and into the room with the sleeping pensioners.

Kerry nervously took Lester's hand. All they could do was watch him go.

XII

"I trust everyone. I just don't trust the devil inside them."

Troy Kennedy Martin

12

Tyler had been gone for about five minutes, but to Kerry it felt like an hour. She knew this was a dangerous idea. To be honest, the entire plan had felt wrong. She should have trusted her gut intuition.

"What's taking him so long?" She asked Lester, who remained beside her, as silent as a church mouse.

"It's only been a few minutes. He may have found something," he responded as reassuringly as he could manage.

He could try to convince Kerry that all would be fine, but he couldn't lie to himself. Lester had been implicated in many of Tyler's hair-brained schemes since childhood and had seen most of them blow up in his face. Sadly for Lester, Tyler had a habit of dragging him down with him. Every time Lester swore he had learned his lesson and yet he always went back for more. Tyler would almost definitely be the death of him.

Kerry was just about to voice how she felt they should just count their losses and run, when, from the bedroom, a loud, shrill scream erupted. Kerry felt her blood run cold. "Oh fuck, no," she said, squeezing Lester's hand so tightly that he pulled it free before she could break it.

Tyler began hollering, loud enough that it got the attention of Shane and Teri downstairs.

"What the fuck?" Teri muttered, but Shane was already on his way up the stairs and hadn't heard her. Teri decided she had better follow.

Shane hit the top of the stairs and saw Kerry and Lester stood looking, anxiously at the bedroom door. "What the fuck was that?" He asked the pair.

"I think they woke up," Kerry answered.

Shane barged into the bedroom, mumbling something about not just standing there.

"Don't you fucking move," Tyler screamed. Shane came running in behind him to find two grey-haired, folks, sat huddled on the bed as Tyler shouted and waved a baseball bat in their faces.

"What the fuck, man?" He said, facing Tyler with a look of complete shock.

"Shut the fuck up, man and help me get these two coffin-dodgers downstairs."

Shane shook his head defiantly. "No way, fuck this dude, let's just leave."

Tyler turned to Shane, a menacing expression crept over his face and Shane instinctively backed up, a couple of steps. Size-wise, Shane had the advantage on Tyler but he knew that his size was no match for Tyler's complete loss of control when pushed.

"We are not going anywhere until we find the cash, and these two know where it is, so like I said. Help me get them downstairs."

Shane nodded in reluctant agreement and walked over to the bed. Taking the old lady under the arm, he hoisted her up on to her feet. "Looks like you're coming with me, Grandma."

"That a boy," Tyler said, heading over to the old man and pulling him to his feet. "You too old fella, you're going to help me find something."

Kerry couldn't believe what she was witnessing. Tyler and Shane emerged from the bedroom, dragging two, frail captives along with them. "What are you doing?" She shouted.

"Everyone, downstairs, now," Tyler yelled back. His tone implied a rage that Lester had hoped to avoid seeing tonight.

Lester pushed past Kerry and seized hold of the back of Tyler's jacket. "We need to leave, now."

With his free hand, Tyler thrust out and grabbed Lester by the throat, shoving him against the bannister. "You don't tell me!" he

yelled in Lester's face. "I tell you. Now get down those fucking stairs." He let go of Lester and continued hauling the old man towards the stairs.

Kerry hurried over to Lester, examining the red handprint left behind by Tyler that now marked his throat. "You fucking prick," she screamed after him.

Tyler ignored her and proceeded down the stairs.

Kerry looked over at Shane. The colour appeared to have drained from his complexion. Teri, however, had a big smile stretched across her face.

"Shane, you need to do something," she implored him.

"Fuck that," he replied. "We need to get out of here."

"You don't know him as we do," Kerry went on. "He's like a shark in a feeding frenzy. Once he gets started, he won't stop. He will hurt those people."

Teri began to chuckle. "This is fucking wild," she spluttered.

"Are you kidding?" Kerry asked, utterly bewildered. "You think this is funny?"

"Fuck yeah," came Teri's reply.

Kerry felt herself snap. She lunged forth, grabbing Teri by the shoulders and forced her hard against the wall. She threw her hand up, ready to slap Teri across the face and would have succeeded, if Lester hadn't caught her and pulled her away. Teri was more than prepared to attack back, had Shane not body blocked her.

Lester took Kerry aside. "Jesus Kerry, calm down."

"That bitch thinks this is amusing. There's nothing funny about Tyler when he gets like this."

"Leave Tyler to me," he said, trying to settle her down. He knew it wouldn't help though. Kerry knew Tyler, or Tyler's kind, all too well.

"Are you as deaf as these old fuckers?" Tyler shouted up the stairs. "I said downstairs, so fucking move it."

XIII

"We all have bad things inside us, and we all choose either to give in to those bad things or to fight them."

Kristin Cast - Untamed

13

By the time everyone made their way downstairs, Tyler had begun securing his newly taken hostages. He hadn't bothered to inform anyone that he had brought a reel of gaffer tape, or rape tape, as he referred to it. Kerry wondered if this had been part of his plan, all along. She wouldn't put it past him. It's as if he got off on situations like this. What concerned her more was that Tyler and Shane had removed their masks. Now the old couple had seen their faces, so now what?

Shane, the wonderful little lapdog that he had become, helped hold the elderly fellow in place, ensuring that he didn't squirm free. Not that Tyler would have objected to an excuse to use a little excessive force. The reason Tyler disliked Kerry so much was that she had clocked him from the very beginning. Kerry could see through all of his bullshit and protest as he might, Tyler just enjoyed hurting people.

As Tyler began fastening the old man's feet together, in a half-hearted act of defiance the old man kicked out, hitting Tyler in the chest. It was a hopeless gesture as there was no actual force behind the blow. Tyler rose to a stand. Grinning at the old man, he belted him across the side of his skull with the back of his hand.

"What the fuck?" Lester called out, outraged by what was taking place.

Tyler ignored him. Leaning closer to the man in the chair, he uttered into his prisoners' ear. "Next time you pull any crap like that, Pop's, I split your old lady's nose. Okay?"

The old man didn't reply; he only nodded. Kerry found something about the look in the man's eyes unsettling. It wasn't fear or even anger. More of a glimmer of satisfaction, although there was no smile to back it up.

Lester had seen enough. He knew precisely where this was heading and if he didn't get a handle on his brother, things would become a lot worse. "Okay, mate, let's just calm things down and think for a minute."

"I am thinking," Tyler answered. "I'm thinking we can't locate the money and that these two know where it is."

"Maybe you're right, but there is a line that we shouldn't cross to find it."

Tyler just chuckled. He had always believed his brother to be weak. "See, that's your problem, Les. You've never had the balls to do what needs to be done, and that's why you always come running to me whenever we do these jobs."

"It has nothing to do with that and you know it."

"It has everything to do with that," Tyler replied. "So I will do what I need to do so we can walk away from here with fatter wallets, and you are either going to help me or stay out of my way."

There was little more that Lester could add. Tyler would never listen to him, and this would play out how Tyler felt it should. No amount of reasoning had ever helped in the past so why should now be any different? He turned to Kerry who was giving him that look that suggested he should try a hell of a lot harder. He just shrugged and shook his head.

Kerry wasn't so easily defeated. "Listen, you do what you need to do but I don't want you hurting anyone, okay?"

"What do you take me for?" Tyler asked.

"You don't want me to answer that," Kerry replied. "Just make it fast so we can get the fuck out of here."

Tyler returned to the old man, bound to the chair. "Okay, Grandpa, we need to talk."

Teri had been watching everything unfold and was loving every minute. This hadn't passed unnoticed. Neither had the fact that she had also removed her mask.

"What are you looking so thrilled about?" Kerry asked.

"What gave me away?"

"Well, for a start, how about that dumb fucking smile on your face," Kerry answered, trying to keep her rage from boiling over. Teri didn't acknowledge. She was more absorbed in what was taking place between Tyler and the inhabitants of the house whose night was going from bad to worse.

"We know old bastards like you don't use bank accounts, so you can show me where you stash your savings."

Shane wasn't convinced they would leave with anything, given how sparse the house was concerning possessions of any kind. He had been through every corner of the residence and had found nothing. They didn't even own a tv. The television was the best friend of the pensioner. Shane knew this to be a fact. His Grandparents, before they had died, wasted hours in front of the goggle box. They claimed that because of a lack of mobility and visitors, television was the next best thing. He put his hand on Tyler's shoulder and leaned in to whisper in his ear. "Can I have a word mate?"

Tyler nodded, and they went over to the end of the room, out of earshot.

"What's up?"

"I think we might be wasting our time," Shane said, nervously assessing Tyler's expression for a sign he may snap. He knew how unpredictable Tyler could be and didn't fancy being on the receiving end of one of his meltdowns.

"What?"

"Look around, dude. They have nothing."

Tyler took an imposing step forward, forcing Shane to back up. Tyler's expression had changed, and it wasn't an encouraging alteration.

"Look, I'm not trying to be a jerk," Shane added, a nervous tremble to his voice now.

"We have spent weeks planning this," Tyler snapped. "You would have us pack up and piss off with nothing?"

"That's not what I mean, but look around man," Shane gestured around the room. "They have fuck all."

Tyler stepped up on Shane again, backing him right into the corner of the room until he bumped the wall. "I say when we give up. These two will help me get what we came for, and you can either help me or remain here and piss your knickers."

"Yeah, okay, sorry man."

Tyler gave Shane a mild slap across the cheek, smiling ominously. "Good boy."

XIV

"The devil's agents may be of flesh and blood, may they
not?"

Arthur Conan Doyle - The Hound of the Baskervilles

14

The thirty-minute maximum, by which they always abide, had been and gone, yet they had so far made zero progress. Something was very wrong within the walls of 232 Jericho Avenue. They all knew it but nobody came forward to address the issue. Where were all the household possessions? Everyone owns things, so why not these two? Old people are hoarders, having collected heirlooms and items of sentimental value over the years. Mr & Mrs Parker, as the group had learnt their names to be, had no such belongings.

It wasn't this that concerned Kerry the most though. Her concerns dwelled more on how The Parkers seemed to react to their plight. After all, they were tied to a chair by a lunatic with a baseball bat. Under normal circumstances, most reasonable people would find this to be most upsetting. Something was very off.

Tyler had been pacing in front of his captives for a good 20 minutes, like a caged Tiger, his aggressive mannerisms making no impact on the bound residents. The longer they held out, the angrier he became. This wasn't typical behaviour. Even Tyler was beginning to suspect there really was nothing of value to be obtained from the house. He would never admit that his tip-off had been phoney though, because that would mean accepting that he had been made a fool of. 'Nobody makes a fool of Tyler Burrows,' he thought.

Mrs Parker watched as he passed back and forth. Her eyes flicked left, then right, fixed on Tyler's every movement. There wasn't an ounce of fright given away in her eyes. To Kerry, it was like watching a Cat as it tracks a bird right before the kill. As far as Kerry was concerned, she may as well have been licking her lips.

Shane and Teri stood across the other side of the room. Everyone had given up searching now, hoping instead that Tyler could break the couple into simply telling them where to look.

Tyler was losing control. He felt his resolve slowly dwindling and that old familiar need to do some damage was taking over him. Could he hurt a couple of pensioners? Even he wasn't sure, but it's not like he had any self-control once the red mist descended.

"We need to do something," Kerry whispered to Lester.
He knew she was right. He knew how bad this could go. What was he meant to do though? When the switch flipped he had about as much control over Tyler as a trainer has over a homicidal Orca at SeaWorld. "Like what?" he asked.
Kerry wasn't sure she knew, but anything had to be better than just standing there. "I don't know, anything," she came back. "Try to reason with them."

Lester nodded and took a few steps towards Tyler and his hostages. "Hi," he said with a hesitant smile.

"What are you doing?" Tyler asked him, a mixture of bewilderment and anger in his voice.

Lester ignored him. "Look, Mr Parker, we don't want anyone getting hurt, so if you can just tell us where you keep all your money we can get going."

Tyler began clapping sarcastically, which caused Shane and Teri to break out laughing. "Now why didn't I think of that?" Tyler asked.

Lester ignored him again and continued. "You don't know my brother and you don't want to, but if you don't help us, I can't protect you."

Mr Parker raised his gaze to meet Lester's and for the first time since waking up to their intruders, he spoke. "Lester isn't it?" He inquired, not blinking. Lester found something about his calm, stony stare unsettling him. It caused the hair along his arms to stand on end.

"Did you tell him my name?" Lester asked his brother who now just looked amazed.

"Of course not," he answered.

"He didn't tell me anything," the old man continued. "I know who you are." The old man still didn't blink. He remained staring as if looking through Lester and into his very soul. "Lester Burrows, brother of Tyler Burrows, Son of Judith and Keith Burrows." Lester looked over to his brother, a look of shock and astonishment painted on his face. The old man kept going. "Beau of Kerry Jones. Lapdog, coward and lackey to his brothers every whim."

"Ok, that's enough," Tyler yelled. Mr Parker didn't flinch. His eyes still burned into Lester's. A smile spread across Mr Parker's face.

Kerry's eyes were now locked on Tyler. He was losing it and something dreadful was going to happen.

"Can't satisfy your girl, can't stand up to your brother," Mr Parker went on. Mrs Parker had now turned to face her husband. An evil smile creeping across her skull too.

"Shut the fuck up you old fool, " Tyler continued yelling, now pointing the bat in his hand directly at Mr Parker's head. Mr Parker finally broke away from staring at Lester and shifted his gaze upon Tyler. Mrs Parker erupted in laughter.

"I'm warning you, you crazy old fucker," Tyler threatened.

"Tyler Burrows," the old man said.

"Shut up man," Tyler said, this time a nervous quiver in his voice. He still pointed the bat, but it did nothing to alarm Mr Parker.

"Bully, thief, wife beater, am I right?" He asked in an accusing tone.

"Seriously, shut the fuck up you crazy old bastard."

Mr Parker chose not to shut up. "You beat your ex-wife so badly she lost the baby she was carrying, am I right?" He flashed Tyler a grin. "You have nothing to offer anyone other than ugliness and violence."

Tyler's hands were shaking as he held the baseball bat out in front of him.

The old man began to shout. "I said, am I right you impotent little faggot?"

All anyone could do at this point was look on in incredulity as the old man goaded Tyler. Everyone except Teri that is. Her eyes widened as if trying to absorb the uncertainty of what might happen next. She didn't look distressed. Her expression was that of someone enjoying a thoroughly terrifying horror movie a little too much.

Tyler continued yelling. Spittle flew from his mouth as the fury inside came bubbling to the surface. "This is your last fucking warning you cunt."

Mr Parker didn't heed this warning. "When's the last time you satisfied a woman you limp dick, fuck?"

Tears of anger streamed down Tyler's cheeks. His grip tightened on the handle of the bat.

"Don't do it Tyler," Kerry called out behind him.

"You beat women because you can't fuck them. Your cock doesn't work so you find other ways of showing them what a man you are. You fucking pussy."

The baseball bat came down with a thud as wood met skull. The first blow was enough to split a gash deep across the old man's scalp. Kerry heard herself cry out in protest but it fell on deaf ears. Mr Parker rocked back in his chair from the blow, causing it to topple backwards, taking him with it.

Kerry charged forwards, hoping to stop anything further from happening, but Lester caught hold of her and dragged her back. She fought to escape his grip, but he was too strong.

Tyler had flipped, and Lester knew that Kerry would get hurt. He wrapped his arms around her still struggling body to restrain her.

Tyler flew round to where the old man's body had landed, still strapped to his chair. One of the chair legs had broken off in the fall, and Tyler kicked it at his lifeless heckler. He began kicking him again and again in the chest, shouting as he did so. Kerry couldn't make out what he was shouting, but she stopped struggling.

Her attention quickly drew to Mrs Parker. Her husband was currently being beaten to death by a thug with a bat, and Mrs Parker was laughing. In fact, she was flat out howling with laughter. Kerry couldn't believe her eyes.

Tyler stopped kicking Mr Parker and began pummelling him with the bat again. A sickening crunching could be heard as the bat rained down repeatedly, fracturing the old man's skull. Each time Tyler lifted the bat, more blood covered it. Mrs Parker continued to laugh hysterically. Kerry wasn't the only one who had noticed this very troubling behaviour now.

Tyler began grunting with exhaustion. His blows grew weaker until he had nothing else to give. His hands and face had become smattered with blood. He dropped the bat and stumbled to the corner of the room. He slid down the wall into a sitting position, breathing heavily.

He motioned to Lester. "Give me a smoke," he said, puffing and panting.

Lester obliged. He reached into his pocket and took out a cigarette, which he passed to Tyler with a shaky hand. Tyler popped the cigarette into his mouth and Lester offered a lighter. His hands shook so badly that he couldn't get it to light. Tyler snatched it from him and lit his smoke.

"What have you done?" Kerry asked, finally finding words.

Tyler ignored her and continued to enjoy his smoke. A look of quiet calm had settled over him as he examined the blood on his hands.

XV

"Society wants to believe it can identify evil people, or bad or harmful people, but it's not practical. There are no stereotypes."

Ted Bundy

15

It must have been five minutes before someone finally spoke. This time it was Shane who broke the silence. "What are we going to do?" He asked.

Tyler, who had finally come back to the land of the living, answered his question. "We're going to find their money," he replied.

Shane looked confused by his response. "Don't you think we should get out of here?"

Tyler started to wipe some blood from his face with his shirt, although it had already started drying so wasn't coming off. "No, I think we need to stay and finish the job."

It was Kerry who chimed in next. She had seen enough and didn't want to spend another minute in the house. "We need to be leaving. If we get caught now, it's not just burglary anymore."

"She's right," Lester added. "You've killed a man Ty. If we get busted now, it's murder."

Tyler sniggered at Lester as if he had cracked a joke. "Nothing's changed Les," he said. "We are still here to do a job, and nobody is leaving until it's done." He pointed over to Mrs Parker. "This bitch is still breathing, and she knows where the money is."

Old lady Parker, who had done laughing hysterically at the brutal murder of her husband some minutes ago, simply smiled at Tyler. "Oh, there is no money honey," she said.

Tyler gestured over to where her deceased husband lay. "Don't play fucking games, old lady, unless you want to end up like your old man."

"Oh, he's alright," she replied.

Tyler might have found her reply strange had it not been that Lester had interrupted. "Come on bro, we should leave."

Tyler grabbed his arm a little harder than Lester would have liked. "No, we are staying. Anyone who tries to leave can join Mr Parker down here."

"I would listen to your brother," the old lady butted in.

"Button it, lady, nobody is talking to you," Lester replied.

Tyler, still gripping his arm, pulled Lester closer and whispered into his ear. "I don't want to hurt anyone else, but you better listen to me, mate. I will stop anyone who doesn't see this through."

Kerry stormed over to where the boys stood arguing. Tonight had gone as bad as it could go and she had had enough. Tyler couldn't stop all of them. "Are we going or not?"

"We are not," Tyler replied.

"You can't hold us all hostage."

"Can't I?" Tyler asked. "You want to test that theory?"

Kerry looked over to Teri, annoyed that she wasn't speaking up. "You want to stay?" She asked.

Teri gave her a satisfied smile. "I'm okay where I am thanks, honey."

Kerry shook her head before turning her attention to Shane. "What about you, muscles?" She asked. "Steroids shrunk your balls?"

It wasn't Shane who answered; it was Mrs Parker. "Oh, you're not going anywhere, little lady," she interrupted.

"I'm sorry?" Kerry asked her.

"Not as fucking sorry as you're going to be," the elderly lady snorted.

Teri began laughing along with her. "That old Witch is crazy," Teri said.

"Listen, lady," Tyler interrupted. "If you don't tell us what we need to know, you will end up as dead as your old man over there." He pointed at the bloodied figure with the caved-in head, laying across the room.

"Oh, he's not dead, dear," Mrs Parker responded. "Give him a minute or two. He's not as young as he used to be."

Tyler gave her a bewildered look. "You really are one crazy old girl."

The old lady wasn't listening. She had started looking around the room. Studying the faces of her uninvited guests. She began murmuring to herself as she did so.

"What's she doing?" Teri asked quietly to Shane who was as mystified as she was. His reply was a shrug. "What are you doing, lady?" She called over to Mrs Parker.

"I'm just putting names to all the faces, my dear," she replied.

Kerry had seen and heard enough. She had felt uneasy about the old woman since Tyler had first dragged them down the stairs and now she wanted answers. "Do you know us?"

"Of course," Mrs Parker replied.

"Care to tell us how?" Kerry pressed.

Another of those creepy smiles appeared on Mrs Parker's face. "I don't think you would like the answer to that question," she said.

"Try me," Kerry countered.

"I know everything about everyone dear."

"What are you, like some superpowered busy-body?" Kerry asked, utterly confounded.

The old woman continued. "I know you, Kerry Jones. I know how you bounced from one foster home to another after your sister died." Mrs Parker had that gleeful look in her eye again, that had bothered Kerry earlier that night. "I know how your sister killed herself after your father raped her. I know how you sometimes think about joining your sister."

Lester took hold of Kerry, wrapping his arm around her shoulder as tears began rolling down her face.

"I wouldn't hurry to join your sister if I were you, young lady," Mrs Parker continued. "Nothing nice awaits you there."

The old lady's last words caused silence to fall over the room. Even Teri who had spent the last half an hour like a grinning idiot expressed a look of shock at what she had just heard fall from the woman's lips.

Kerry staggered back, tears welling in her eyes, and Lester reached out to embrace her. She shrugged him away and took a seat at the other side of the living room, taking steps to compose herself. She wasn't going to let this weird bitch get to her.

It was Lester who broke the silence. He had been taking it all in. Trying to figure out what was going on and how this old cow could know so much about a bunch of people she had never met.

"Who the fuck are you?" Was all he could think to say. To everyone's surprise, old lady Parker never answered. Instead, she folded her arms across her chest and began to sing.

"Oh, the weather outside is frightful, but the fire is so delightful. And since we've no place to go, let it snow, let it snow, let it snow.."

"What the fuck is she doing?" Teri asked to anybody who was listening. She didn't get an answer. The old lady continued singing away as if nobody else was in the room.

"It doesn't show signs of stopping, but we've brought some corn for popping. The lights are turned way down low. Let it snow, let it snow, let it snow.."

With everyone's attention on the crazy old lady, nobody noticed the strange twitching that the arm belonging to the man with the smashed in skull had started doing. Even Tyler, who was mere feet from the mess he had created with Mr Parker, was oblivious, due to Mrs Parker's impromptu entertainment.

The fingers on the dead man's hand began to flex as if trying to grip something that wasn't there. This would have seemed very strange, had anyone actually observed it.

Mrs Parker finally finished her song and then gleefully started to applaud herself. Nobody knew for sure how she was no longer bound to the chair. She finished clapping, and the smile disappeared from her face as fast as it had appeared. "Sorry dear, what was the question?"

Tyler had had enough. He leapt to his feet and was just about to launch himself at the old lady when a small lamp went barrelling past him and hit the wall. The shade on the lamp buckled, and the bulb smashed on impact.

"What the fuck?" Was all that sprang from his mouth. He stopped in his tracks and turned to where he figured the lamp had begun its journey.

A small standing table that had housed the lamp lay at the feet of Mr Parker's corpse. Its leg, broken. If Tyler didn't know any better, he would swear it looked as if the corpse had kicked it over.

Instinctively he leaned in closer to examine the table and as he did, the corpse of old man Parker kicked the broken table hard against the wall. Tyler jumped back in terror, his heart beating so hard in his chest he felt sure it would break his ribs.

Tyler wasn't alone. Everyone jumped. Everyone except the old lady. That sinister grin returned to her face. "Oh, you're all in trouble now," she said.

Lester could only find it in him to repeat his brother's last sentiment. "What the fuck?"

Tyler scanned the room. "You all just saw that right?" he asked.

"That's not normal," Teri added.

They all stood, frozen to the spot, watching. Waiting. After what felt like an eternity, but realistically could only have been seconds, the arms on Mr Parker's corpse began to spasm. Only slightly at first and then they picked up momentum until they were thrashing wildly.

At this point, everyone made a dash for the other side of the room. Everyone except Kerry, who was almost bowled over in the stampede.

As everyone huddled the wall, Shane had seen enough. Without even stopping to suggest that Teri join him, he made a bee-line towards the hallway.

"Where do you think you're going, big boy?" Mrs Parker challenged.

"I'm getting the fuck out of here," he replied, without looking back.

"Ok, good luck with that, maggot," the old lady responded.

Shane shot across the hallway to the front door. The only problem he had now was that there wasn't a front door. Exasperated, he pounded his hands against the solid wall where the door should have been. With his escape cut off, he searched the house for another means of escape. There wasn't one. No doors. No windows. There had been at one time but now, all the house offered was wall.

Overwhelmed by the sudden events of the evening, Shane stormed back into the room. He marched over to the old lady and without saying a word, punched her in the nose. She rocked back in her chair, blood exploding from her nostrils. The smile never left her face. The corpse in the corner of the room continued to thrash as if an electrical current coursed through it. Still, nobody said a word.

XVI

"Darkness always had its part to play. Without it, how would we know when we walked in the light? It's only when its ambitions become too grandiose that it must be opposed, disciplined, sometimes—if necessary—brought down for a time. Then it will rise again, as it must."

Clive Barker - Abarat

16

Sean checked his phone for what felt like the hundredth time. 'It never takes this long,' he thought to himself. He knew how they operated, and he knew they only usually took 30 minutes to get in and get out. Tyler always sent a message once they were home free but, two hours later, he had heard nothing.

He considered calling, but it seemed like a bad idea. Breaking protocol would only serve to incur Tyler's wrath and he didn't need that. Maybe if he sent a text message, just in case. That wouldn't go against the grain, would it? He opened his phone again and began to type. As his fingers hit the keys, he had an epiphany. "What the fuck am I doing?" He asked himself.

Repeatedly the brothers had demonstrated their contempt for Sean and the job he performed. He knew that should the shit hit the fan, they wouldn't care if he was dragged down with them. Yet he had always put his neck on the line to ensure that they were ok.

He stopped typing and put his phone back into his pocket. 'Fuck them,' he thought as he turned his attention to getting himself another cup of coffee.

Could he really leave them out to hang or was it a case of momentary bravado? He would mull it over while he enjoyed his hot cup of wake up juice.

XVII

"Most of us have learned to be dispassionate about evil, to look it in the face and find, as often as not, our own grinning reflections with which we do not argue, but good is another matter. Few have stared at that long enough to accept that its face too is grotesque, that in us the good is something under construction. The modes of evil usually receive worthy expression. The modes of good have to be satisfied with a cliche or a smoothing down that will soften their real look."

Flannery O'Connor

17

Events inside the house were growing stranger by the second. Being socked in the nose had done nothing to silence old lady Parker. Having composed herself and used her tongue to drink down as much of the nose blood as she could get at, she had decided that what everyone needed was another Christmas song. So, while her uninvited guests had pulled themselves together enough to start searching frantically for a way out of their new prison, the crazy woman had treated them to a rendition of Silent Night.

The motivation to find an escape had come to them all the minute the old man's body had stopped thrashing and twitching and appeared to be melting into the carpet. They had watched, mouths agape, as steam began to hiss from little pockets that opened in the skin. As the steam escaped, the flesh began to bubble before taking on the characteristics of a candle left too close to a heat source. It fizzed and oozed as it dissolved.

As the smell had hit their nostrils, Shane had doubled over and evacuated the contents of his stomach. All the others just ran in all directions. They had seen enough and just wanted out.

They all discovered the terrifying truth that Shane had uncovered not many minutes before. There was no way out. The house had somehow sealed itself into a tomb and had no intention of releasing the intruders.

"Where's the fucking door?" Tyler shouted as he pounded the solid walls.

Lester wanted to answer but had no idea how to offer an explanation. None of this made sense.

Kerry began kicking against the wall as hard as she could under the illusion that she might kick herself free. She figured it could be some trickery involving boards or something similar. It wasn't. The walls that had replaced their only means of escape were solid brick. "What are we meant to do now?" She said, reeling from the pain that now shot up her ankle.

As she bent down to examine the damage she had caused herself, Lester came over to check her out. "Is it bad?" he asked with genuine concern.

Kerry winced when her hands made contact with the now swelling ankle. She shrugged it off and attempted to stand up. "It's ok. It's not bad."

Lester helped her to her feet, and she hobbled over to lean on the bannister at the foot of the stairs. "What are we going to do, Les?" Her voice trembled with a mix of fear and pain.

"I don't know. We need to get out of here somehow."

Their conversation was abruptly interrupted by screaming that burst forth from the living area. Giving no thought to what they might find, the four of them rushed back into the room, Lester almost carrying the badly limping Kerry. They could never have expected what they were about to find.

Mrs Parker sat cackling like a witch. Beside her stood her once-dead husband. Not 20 minutes ago he had been a headless pulp of bone and blood and yet, here he stood, as if his slaying had never taken place.

The old man was completely naked. What appeared to be an oily substance covered his wrinkled old body. He held his arm extended outwards, his hand gripped firmly around Shane's throat. He was strong. Ridiculously strong as Shane's feet were no longer in contact with the floor, his face turning purple and his eyes bulging desperately as the life was being choked from him. The old man watched as his audience arrived, his face filled with malice as he addressed Tyler. "That fucking hurt you little cunt," he spat.

"Jesus Christ," was all that Kerry's brain would allow her to say.

The naked old man fixed his cold black eyes on her. "Not in this fucking house," he responded.

He turned his attention back to the body in his hand that was beginning to go limp. "As for you, you big fucker, it's time to say goodnight." The newly reanimated Mr Parker gave a flick of the wrist and broke Shane's neck. A loud crack rang out as he did so, and as a piece of bone burst through the flesh, Mr Parker achieved an erection.

All Kerry could hear was Teri's shrill scream. It sounded just like the scream that haunted her repeating nightmare and it caused a cold shiver to run up her spine. Still, her eyes never left the events that unfolded in front of her.

The old man threw Shane's lifeless body to the floor. It landed with a dull thud. He turned to his wife, whose eyes were now fixed on his engorged member. "You're so getting fucked later Albert, you nasty old bastard," she said excitedly. Mr Parker just laughed at her outburst.

Albert, as he was known to his wife, decided he had best address the rest of the room. As he took a stride towards the group, they backed away, not wanting to be anywhere close to this deranged, geriatric lunatic.

"What the hell are you?" Kerry found the courage to ask.

"Why I'm just an old man," he responded. "A frail, vulnerable, old man that you little shits decided to prey upon."

Tyler began to try to speak, but the slowly approaching Albert was having none of it. "You parasitic, over-developed cum-stains think you can do as you please, you assume that ordinary folk are here for you to fuck over." He wiped the drool that spilt from his mouth with the back of his hand. "Well, guess what? We are not ordinary people, and you cockroaches are all going to die."

As he lunged forward, everyone instinctually darted out of the way. Teri wasn't so lucky. Albert Parker caught a handful of her hair and yanked her off her feet. He then dragged her back over towards his still seated wife. Tyler seized the opportunity and ran up behind Albert's turned back and, with as much force as he could summon, threw a punch right into the back of old Albert's head. Having no effect whatsoever, Albert turned and countered, punching Tyler in the oesophagus. Stumbling backwards, Tyler fell hard against the wall. He grasped desperately at his throat, trying to breathe.

Kerry came to him, inspecting his red, swollen neck as he spluttered, taking panicked gulps of air. If anyone had told Kerry yesterday that she would be rushing to comfort Tyler, she would have thought they were joking. Yet here she was, embracing him. Trying to calm him down so he could draw breath.

Albert positioned the struggling Teri in front of his wife and with a swift kick to the back of the knees, she fell to the floor. "Have something to play with Evelyn," he said as if presenting his wife with a gift.

Mrs Parker, or Evelyn, as her name was revealed to be, leaned forward in her chair and began stroking the hair of the sobbing girl in front of her. "Why all the tears child?" She asked. "Everything was so amusing to you not so long ago."

The tears continued to stream down Teri's face. She couldn't bring herself to look up at the old lady, much less respond to her question.

"Oh, I understand," Evelyn continued. "Is it because my husband broke your bastard boyfriend's neck?"

Again, she didn't answer. She just sat, slumped at the old woman's feet, shaking with fright and flinching every time she felt those disgusting nails that protruded from Evelyn's fingers touch her skin.

Frustrated by her lack of reply, Evelyn grabbed a fistful of Teri's hair and yanked her head back, forcing Teri to make eye contact with her.

"I liked you better when you had some balls about you," she snarled in Teri's face. "What happened to your boyfriend will seem merciful, compared to what we have in store for you, piggy."

Albert Parker stood with his hands on his hips, groin thrust proudly forward so as to draw attention to his still erect penis. "I think the cat has her tongue honey."

Evelyn began stroking Teri's face, very tenderly so as not to mark her with her unsightly nails. "I think it's all this metal shit in her face. Maybe her lips are too heavy."

Albert laughed. "Well, why not do the decent thing and help the girl out?" He suggested.

Evelyn Parker nodded at her husband's advice. She continued stroking Teri's tear-soaked face. Her hand brushed gently across her cheek towards her mouth. She paused momentarily before hooking her finger in through one of Teri's lip rings. She gripped it tightly and then pulled.

Teri cried out in pain as the metal ring was torn through the flesh of her mouth.

XVIII

"Unless a man becomes the enemy of an evil, he will not
even become its slave but rather its champion."

G.K. Chesterton

18

By the time Evelyn had ripped out the eighth ring from her lips, Teri had passed out. The lower half of her once pretty face now resembled the shredded doner meat that packed kebabs. As the old lady sat, idly flicking the flaps of flesh that was once Teri's mouth, as if now bored because her plaything had become unconscious, her still very naked husband had taken to tormenting the rest of the uninvited callers. "You all really screwed up tonight, didn't you?"

Nobody answered. Nobody knew how to answer. Shock had a way of shutting down even the loudest of voices.

Albert Parker didn't require an answer. It was a sermon he was delivering, not a pop-quiz. "You thought, let's go rip these old folks off. It will be easy pickings. Yet here you sit, huddled and afraid. One of you is already dead. One of you wishes she was dead and..." he looked into the faces of the three cowering members of his congregation. "well, you will be joining the other two soon enough."

"Bored now," his wife called over. "Why don't you tell them who we are?" She suggested.

"What, and spoil the surprise?" He replied.

"They don't care about the surprise," she responded. "Look at them. They want answers. Poor little lambs."

Albert rolled his eyes. "Fine, "he muttered. "Ok, pay attention rodents. I'm going to school you in a few home truths."

Evelyn began to clap with joy. She loved this part. "I want to wake this thing up before you start," she said, shaking Teri to rouse her from her slumber.

"She isn't waking up honey," Albert said.

"Give me a second here. I'm pretty sure I can get her attention."

Albert looked back over at his audience. He at least had their attention. "Women," he said, shaking his head. "They never bloody listen."

"I heard that," Evelyn snapped.

The old lady had coerced a groan from Teri, but little more. She wasn't coming round any time soon and Albert's composure had worn thin. Evelyn Parker had given up trying and had taken to once again playing with the meat that hung where Teri's mouth should be.

"So," Albert began. "Did any of you kids go to Sunday school?"

His question went unanswered. He let that slide and continued. "Well, as anyone who studied religious education would tell you, there is a special place for people who break the rules. For those who ignore the commandments set by God himself, if you believe in such a fella. For those who steal, kill and generally act like a bunch of fuckhead's. Basically, people like you."

Kerry watched as the drool began to spill from the old man's mouth once again. It ran down his chin and dripped onto his bare chest with a revolting splash that made her want to throw up.

The old man continued. "Generally, you're meant to die before you're judged and sent off to this special place. You idiots got here a little early."

Kerry found enough courage to finally speak up. "You mean Hell, right?"

Albert applauded her question. "Straight to the top of the class for you young lady," he responded with a cheer.

Despite their dilemma, Kerry managed a slight smile at this notion. "So, this is Hell? And I'm guessing that makes you The Devil?"

Albert Parker grabbed a chair and sat himself down in front of Kerry and the others. As he did so, his legs spread, making it impossible for her not to make eye contact with his genitalia. This did nothing to alleviate the nausea that caused her stomach to do somersaults.

"Do you know what an event horizon is?" He asked, focusing on Kerry now, over the others.

"Yes of course," she replied snarkily.

"Go on," he pushed for an answer.

Kerry couldn't help but wish that she had kept her mouth shut. The old man was now locked on her and her alone, and she didn't like it one bit. "It's the boundary around a black hole where nothing can escape. Not even light."

Albert turned to his wife. A big smile on his face. "Did you hear that, honey? We have a smarty pants on our hands. I like this girl." He turned his attention back to Kerry. "You're clearly very bright."

"It's basic physics knowledge, she replied. "What does that have to do with anything, anyway?"

"Think of this house as an event horizon," Albert answered. "A point in the universe where you are going to be sucked into a black hole and there is no escape. This isn't the black hole itself, however, this is just the gateway."

It was Tyler who spoke next, his voice weak and croaky due to the damage inflicted on his throat. He forced his words out. The cost was instant anguish, and he grimaced as he spoke them. "What's he talking about Kerry?"

The old man switched his attention to Tyler. A look of seething hatred washed over him as he did so. "Ah the thug speaks," he said. "What do you understand about any of this?"

Tyler didn't answer. He didn't get the question. He stared back at the old man blankly.

Albert continued. "Do you believe in God?" he asked him.

Kerry spoke up in Tyler's place. "No, of course not," came her reply.

The old man laughed. "Good, as well you should not. He doesn't believe in you either. He hasn't for some time now."

Kerry managed a laugh this time. What she was hearing seemed absurd. It shouldn't. They were trapped in a house because the doors and windows had vanished. She had seen Tyler beat a man to death, only to have him return, completely unscathed. That same, very old man had lifted a two-hundred-pound man in the air and snapped his neck like a twig. Yet here she sat, still questioning the credibility of anything that he said, and why wouldn't she? Everything he said sounded ridiculous. "You didn't answer my question," she interrupted.

Albert cast her a smile that lightened his features for a fleeting moment. "What question was that sweetie?"

"I asked if you were The Devil?" She repeated.

Albert let out a loud, obnoxious laugh. This, in turn, caused Evelyn to stop what she was doing and laugh along with him. "You hear that Evie? She thinks I'm The Devil."

"Watch how you flatter him, dear," Evelyn said. "He's a sucker for that kind of thing."

The laughter subsided and Albert's features took on a more sinister expression. He stared deeply into Kerry's eyes and she felt trapped by it. Try as she might to evade his gaze, she just couldn't divert her eyes from his. He had latched onto her and it was inescapable.

"No, silly. To answer your question, I'm not The Devil. I'm not even sure there is a Devil." He wiped the drool from his chin with his arm. It was a pointless gesture as it was immediately replaced with another stream. "If there is, I haven't met him."

Still unable to look away from his piercing, pale blue eyes, Kerry struggled to form the words she needed to ask the questions that buzzed around her brain. She felt hypnotised. Like she had somehow become hijacked and was losing control of herself. She managed to spit her next question out, but it took real effort. "So, what are you then?" The words came spluttering from her mouth and she wasn't even sure they were in the right order.

The old man could see that she was struggling. Of course, she was struggling. He had entered her soul and had begun to feed. It always took a toll on the recipient. It wasn't fatal. Well, not over the short period of time Albert required to feed off her, anyway. Sure, prolonged exposure to his feeding would result in death, but Albert just needed a boost. Regenerating after having his head removed with a baseball bat was draining. He needed a pick me up and Kerry was the unsuspecting vendor.

XIX

"Most people are good and occasionally do something they know is bad. Some people are bad and struggle every day to keep it under control. Others are corrupt to the core and don't give a damn, as long as they don't get caught. But evil is a completely different creature, Mac. Evil is bad that believes it's good."

Karen Marie Moning - Shadowfever

19

Was it curiosity or concern that had gotten the best of him? Sean wasn't so sure. Either way, he had to know what had happened. As tempted as he had been to shrug it off as 'not his problem' there was no way his conscience would let him off that easy.

He had made some excuse to the boys back at the station before getting into his car and driving to Jericho Avenue. He figured that he could put his mind at rest by performing a drive-by. Maybe, in all the excitement, they had simply forgotten to let him know that they were home free. More likely, they hadn't deemed him important enough to keep informed.

As his car arrived at his destination, the sight of Lester's van, still parked in front of the green, caused his heart to sink into his stomach. 'Oh shit,' he thought, 'they're still inside.'
Sean pulled the car up a few feet behind the van and switched his engine off. He needed to consider his options. Something had obviously gone very wrong as it was now three in the morning and they should have been long gone.

He pulled his phone from his pocket and unlocked it, but there was still no message from Tyler. Usually, he would consider the old adage that no news was good news, but he highly doubted that it applied here.

Reaching into the glove compartment of his car, Sean retrieved the pack of cigarettes he kept hidden from his wife. He had quit a couple of years back but the stress of the job, coupled with the added responsibility of being a new father, had turned him into a sneaky smoker. At first, he figured he could get by with the odd, crafty puff, but as time rolled on, he found himself making excuses just to get out of the house so he could fill his lungs with the sweet, stress-relieving nicotine. No amount of nicotine would calm him now, though. A fact that was sadly re-enforced as he sucked down the thick, grey poison.

"Come on guys, give me a clue," he said to himself before expelling the smoke from his lungs. It danced across the dashboard like a cold, heavy winter mist.

Sean checked his phone one last time before flicking his smoke out through the gap in the window. 'Fuck it,' he thought. 'I'm going to go look.'

XX

"Justice, like beauty, is in the eye of the beholder. Some see an innocent victim. Others will see evil incarnate getting exactly what's deserved."

Emily Thorne

20

Albert Parker stood, legs apart, arms outstretched, and he felt fantastic. A little soul food had been just what he needed after having had his brains mulched into a paste. The process had had quite the opposite effect on Kerry, however, who was now out cold.

There had been an outburst of protest from Lester during the procedure. He had taken it upon himself to stop the old man, even though he wasn't sure exactly what the old man was doing. He knew from the effect it was having on Kerry that it wasn't good. His interference had cost him a tooth as Albert had struck him in the mouth with a strength that someone of his age shouldn't possess.

He had looked on in horror as Albert had pulled his lost tooth from his wrinkled knuckle and then proceeded to put it into his mouth and swallow it. As blood flowed from his swollen mouth, the site of the old man eating his now missing tooth caused him to retch, which in turn made him to choke on his own blood.

The sight of Lester coughing and spluttering and spraying mouth blood down his chest incited gleeful clapping and cheering from Albert before he dropped down onto the palms of his hands and began performing press-ups. He pounded out one after another with an ease usually reserved for someone a third of his age.

Evelyn couldn't resist the sight of her husband's showing off. She shoved Teri, who up till now had been her primary point of interest, with enough force that her head made a sickening crunch as it connected with the floor. A trickle of blood began to form and soak into the pea-green carpet.

Evelyn stood and began rubbing her hands together, feasting her eyes on Albert's bare arse as it pumped up and down.

She licked her lips and started heading towards her husband. "I'm going to have me a little taste of that arsehole."

She positioned herself behind her husband and placed her hands on the cheeks of his behind and slowly began parting them. As she lowered her head the sudden, piercing chimes of Big Ben encroached on the little treat she had planned for her husband.

Albert stopped mid-press-up. Everyone except Kerry who hadn't come around yet flung their heads in the direction of the hallway, where the noise had come from.

Albert took to his feet. "Who the fuck could that be, ringing the doorbell at this hour?"

Tyler and Lester opened their mouth's ready to sound off with cries for help, but as they did so they realised that try as they might, no sound would leave their lips. They looked at each other, wide-eyed with panic and confusion over suddenly being rendered mute.

Evelyn got to her feet and addressed the two of them. "Don't go getting all worked up," she said. "We can't very well have you squealing like a couple of big girls." She looked over to her annoyed-looking husband. "You stay here and keep an eye on these germs. You can't very well go answering the door with your flag flying."

Albert looked down at his now semi-erect penis and laughed. "Yes dear, of course."

XXI

"In any compromise between food and poison, it is only death that can win. In any compromise between good and evil, it is only evil that can profit."

Ayn Rand

21

As the door to 232 was opened, the intensity from the hallway light took Sean by surprise. He shielded his eyes from the glare to let them adjust. He could just about make out the figure of the old lady as his vision slowly fought to focus.

The old lady looked at the new arrival, a look of disdain on her face. "Yes? What do you mean, calling at this time of night?"

Sean lowered his hand and replied to her agitated question. "I'm sorry to disturb you, madam. I'm with the police." He handed her his identification, and she glanced over it before handing it back.

"We've had a few reports of disturbances in the area and I just wanted to call by to check that you were ok and to ask if you'd seen anything untoward?"

"It's very late, you know?" she replied. "My husband and I were asleep."

"I Know, madam. Once again, I'm very sorry for the intrusion."

Evelyn wasn't stupid, not by a long shot and she knew that this visit from the constabulary wasn't a coincidence. Clearly, her and Albert's activities with their visitors had thrown any plans for a rendezvous out of sync, and this imbecile thought he could pull the wool over her eyes with some concocted story about neighbourhood disturbances.

Sean pushed again for an answer. "So, is everything ok, madam?"

She thought over how best to deal with this situation for a second before answering. "Well, I didn't want to make a fuss, but we had some kids try to break in earlier tonight. They smashed a window but my husband heard them and he must have scared them off when he came downstairs."

'Maybe they hadn't made it inside,' he thought. 'Maybe they had actually been scared off.' He smiled at the frail-looking old woman. "Why didn't you call us earlier?" he asked.

"Oh, we didn't want to make a fuss. They soon ran off, and it's only a window. We called our Son and he said if we covered it over he would come out and fix it first thing. He's very good to us."

Sean offered her another smile. "I'm sure he is madam, but sleeping with a broken window isn't exactly safe. Mind if I come in and take a look?"

Evelyn hesitated for a moment before responding. "I don't want to be any trouble."

"It's no trouble," Sean replied. "It's all part of the job."

"Ok, well, if you insist. What a lovely young man you are."

She stepped aside to let Sean enter. "It's my pleasure, madam," he said as he entered the hallway. "Which window did you say it was?"

116

Evelyn pointed to the door that led into the living room. "It's just through there," she answered. An evil smile crept over her face. "Lead the way young man."

Sean did as instructed. He made his way to the door at the end of the hall and pushed it open.

As he stood there taking it all in, Sean found himself rooted to the spot. He couldn't begin to comprehend what he had walked into. His cousins sat, huddled and bleeding in the room's corner. Pressed up against the flowered wallpaper that would look more at home in an East End pub than a home. Kerry lay on the carpet and he couldn't make out if she was dead or just sleeping. The body of some guy that Sean had never seen before was sprawled out over the other side of the room. He was definitely dead. Nobody's head should twist at that angle. Worst of all was the girl whose face appeared to have been shredded.

He opened his mouth to address the situation but barely a sound left his lips before a hand exploded through the back of his head. His eyeballs erupted from their sockets. Forced out by the two fingers that pushed their way through his skull.

Sean was dead before he even knew what had hit him. Evelyn stood behind him cackling, wiggling her hand around inside Sean's head. She lingered for a moment before pulling her blood and brain-soaked hand free. Sean's lifeless body crumbled to the floor.

"Call me madam, you patronising cunt," she said, giving the body a swift kick.

Tyler heard screaming. He was totally unaware that it was coming from Lester. He couldn't compose a thought. All he could do was sit, glued to the spot in abject terror.

XXII

"God never talks. But the devil keeps advertising, Father. The devil does a lot of commercials."

William Peter Blatty - The Exorcist

22

Kerry sat nursing the worst headache she had ever known. She felt groggy, like she had just come round from having had anaesthetic. She was, as yet, clueless as to what had taken place over the last half an hour. Rubbing her throbbing temples, she desperately tried to convince her eyes to focus on her surroundings. She could hear crying. A girl crying. Teri?

Teri was now very conscious and in a great deal of pain, her once beautiful face now ruined. She sobbed uncontrollably and the salty tears that ran down her face caused the exposed raw meat that replaced her mouth to sting.

Her crying had attracted the attention of Evelyn who returned to once again give Teri her undivided attention. Evelyn cradled Teri, whispering her reassurances that everything would be fine and that she wouldn't have to suffer for much longer. Well, not in this world anyway.

Tyler had finally managed to pull himself together and had spent the last few minutes weighing up his options. A few feet from where he sat, lay the broken table leg that had snapped off during Albert's weird, twitchy corpse episode. It looked sharp, almost stake like. If he could just make it over there in time, he was sure he could use it to attack his captors and get the rest of them out of there.

If he was going to act, it needed to be now. Evelyn was preoccupied with Teri and Albert had finally decided to go and get some clothes on. 'Even if I manage to take them out of the picture, how am I meant to leave the house?' he thought. 'There are no fucking doors.'

Evelyn wasn't looking and Albert was nowhere to be seen. Tyler was going for it. Slowly he moved into a crouched position and made ready for the off. He felt a hand on his arm. It was Lester who was wide-eyed and shaking his head. Tyler took hold of Lester's hand and gave it a gentle squeeze before pushing it aside. He gave Lester a half-hearted smile before springing into action.

It all happened so fast that even Tyler couldn't believe how quickly he had achieved it. He sprinted as fast as he could over to the broken table leg. Grasping it, and bringing it up to his chest, he spun around and noticed Evelyn rising from her kneeling position next to Teri. Without missing a beat he launched himself towards her and drove the wooden leg deep into the socket of her eye. He delivered the blow with such force that the leg went clean through, breaking free through the back of her head. Bits of brain tissue and bloody membrane hung from the pointy end as it emerged.

As Evelyn dropped back onto her knees she let out a deafening, high-pitched squeal, forcing everyone to clamp their hands over their ears.

Tyler wasn't done yet. His eyes rested on the discarded baseball bat that he had thrown aside after attacking Albert with it earlier. He seized possession of it and ran back over to the still screeching Evelyn.

He stood over her and lifted the bat high above his head. "Shut the fuck up you crazy fucking witch." It was the only remotely cool thing he could think to say as the adrenaline surged through him. He suddenly felt invincible. He could do this and he could get them all to safety.

The bat came crashing down on the top of Evelyn's head. Her skull parted almost immediately, and she slumped to the floor, suddenly quiet. Tyler lifted the bat for a second strike, but it never came. He never saw the old man coming at him, but he felt the impact. As he hit the deck, Tyler felt like a car had struck him.

Albert was on top of him, raining down blows before he had time to think. Thinking had never been Tyler's strong point. He was more inclined to react, and his instinct to fight back was where he excelled. He thrust his hands up to Albert's face. Griping the sides of his head, Tyler thrust his thumbs into Albert's eyes. He heard a squelchy, popping sound as his digits forced their way through the eyeballs and black fluid cascaded down his hands and wrists.

Blinded, Albert leaped off of Tyler and tripped over the seat that his wife had spent much of her evening sitting in. He rolled around, screaming, clutching at he mangled sockets that had once housed his eyes.

Tyler jumped to his feet and ran over to where a still rather groggy Kerry sat. He grabbed her by the neck of her hooded top and hoisted her to her feet before turning to his brother. "Get up, Les. We are leaving."

Lester didn't need to be told twice. He couldn't quite believe that Tyler had managed to take them both out, but he wasn't going to sit around and question what had taken place. He was on his feet in no time and they all rushed out into the hallway in a bid for freedom.

XXIII

"Sin, death, and hell have set their marks on him,
And all their ministers attend on him."

William Shakespeare - Richard III

23

Freedom, it seemed would not come easy. Once again, the doors and windows had vanished, leaving only a wall.

"It's a trick," Kerry said. " It has to be. There was a door here when they let Sean in."

Lester agreed. "This has to be a trick, or maybe some panel that slides over to hide the door. Maybe there is a lever or something."

Tyler wasn't interested in looking for a lever. He had a better idea and bolted to the staircase.

"What are you doing?" Kerry called after him.

Tyler stopped briefly to answer her question. "I'm going upstairs. We didn't bother checking last time and for all we know, the windows upstairs could still be there." With that, he turned and raced up the stairs, two at a time.

She had to admit it, he made a compelling point. She took hold of Lester and started towards the stairs. Her ankle still throbbed, but she wasn't going to let that slow her down. 'God only knows how long it will be before those old fuckers would be fighting fit and after them again,' she thought. She wasn't going to hang around and find out.

Back in the living room, Evelyn's corpse had gone through the motions of twitching and gyrating and had now commenced dissolving into the carpet much like her husband's had previously.

Albert, however, had taken a seat. He figured he would wait out the inevitable return of his vision. He wasn't sure exactly how long it would take. He hadn't lost his eyes before, but it surely wouldn't be too long before he could watch the rest of them die. 'They are going to die, slowly and painfully,' he thought.

Teri couldn't believe they had abandoned her. She was in no fit state to have joined their escape of her own free will. She wasn't even sure she could stand. She was a complete mess. The damage done to her mouth had caused her face to swell. On top of all her other troubles, she could barely see. Her puffy eyes were constantly filled with water. 'I'm going to die on this ugly carpet,' was as close to a coherent thought as she could get.

Tyler had been right. The windows upstairs remained a permanent feature of the house. He punched the air victoriously as the other two hurried to join him in the main bedroom. "I fucking told you," he said.

"Thank fuck," Kerry added. "Let's get out of here.

Tyler slid the latch over and hoisted the window up. He was met with a cold rush of air from outside and in that moment, Tyler was sure he had never felt anything more rewarding and perfect.

"Wait," Lester called out. "We're upstairs. How are we getting down?"

Tyler hadn't thought that far ahead. He looked out of the window, considering his options. "Fuck it," he decided. "I'm just going to drop."

"You're going to drop?" Kerry asked. Astonished by how little thought he had given it. "You'll break your legs."

"Don't be ridiculous," Tyler mocked. "It's not that far. We can do this."

Lester nodded in agreement. "We don't have much choice and we definitely don't have much time. Even if we hurt ourselves, at least we are finally outside."

"That's right," Tyler agreed. " We can worry about any injuries we suffer once we are far away from here.

She hated to admit it, but they were right. They had very little in the way of options. "Ok, fine. Who's first?" she asked.

Tyler was already preparing to exit the room. "I'll go first," he said. "If I land safely then we'll know that you two should be ok."

They both nodded in agreement and Tyler took that as a sign to go. He climbed out of the window and, still gripping the sill, lowered himself down as far as his outstretched arms would allow. 'Here goes fuck all,' he thought, and with that, he let go.

XXIV

"The dark is generous, and it is patient, and it always wins.
It always wins because it is everywhere.
It is in the wood that burns in your hearth, and in the kettle
on the fire; it is under your chair and under your table and
under the sheets on your bed. Walk in the midday sun, and the
dark is with you, attached to the soles of your feet.
The brightest light casts the darkest shadow."

Matthew Stover

24

It didn't make any sense. He couldn't understand how one minute, he was hanging outside of the open window, and the next, sat on his arse inside of the bedroom while Lester and Kerry gawked at him, open-mouthed and speechless.

They had watched him exit the window. They had seen him lower himself into position, and they had watched with bated breath as he had released his grip, only to appear right in front of where they stood. Back in the fucking house.

"How the fuck?" Kerry managed. Not quite completing her question. Something had interrupted her thought process.

Muffled voices could be heard coming from downstairs. It sounded like the owners.

"It's happened again," Kerry said. "She's back."

They all leaned forward as if that would somehow aid them in hearing who the voices belonged to. It was a futile and foolish gesture as it made no difference.

"I'm going again," Tyler said before climbing back out of the window. This time, rather than dangle, he jumped. He figured he would just roll out the momentum once he hit the floor. The floor he hit was the one he had just left. Once again he was back in the bedroom.

"This doesn't make any fucking sense," he shouted, frustrated.

Kerry and Lester couldn't agree more.

The old lady stood naked. Her skin gleamed in the light. Covered in the same oily substance that had coated her husband on his return. She walked over to Albert who was shielding his new eyeballs from the glare of the bulb that hung, unshaded, in the middle of the ceiling.

Evelyn embraced her husband who, still squinting through light sensitivity, found another use for his hands. He ran them all over her greasy, naked flesh, rubbing himself against her as he did so. As his hands snaked down to her bare, slippery arse, he plunged his tongue deep into her mouth.

Tyler had quietly made his way out to the top of the stairs to confirm that the Parker's were very much up and active. He would never know how lucky he was that he couldn't see into the living room from that position. The sight of Mr and Mrs Parker hammering into one another would have been too much for anyone to have to process.

Once satisfied that they were both there, he moved quickly to let Lester and Kerry know that they needed to find somewhere to hide. 'But hide where?' he thought. The house was big, but it was hardly Addams Family big.

"I saw an access hatch for the loft," Kerry whispered. "If we can get up there without being seen, it could buy us some time to think."

Tyler nodded in agreement. "That's a good idea. You keep a lookout and we can get the hatch open."

"I'm not sure I think that's the best idea," Lester chimed in. "We're basically cornering ourselves."

"Then suggest something better," Kerry challenged him.

Lester's silence was all they needed to know, he had no better solution.

"It's settled then. We're going up into the loft," Tyler concluded.

With that, Tyler and Kerry made their way out of the bedroom leaving Lester little option but to follow.

Kerry positioned herself at the top of the stairs. She didn't have a clear visual on the where-abouts of the old couple, but she didn't need one. The moaning sounds coming from the front room as the Parkers copulated like a couple of horny teenagers was enough to alert her to the fact that they weren't being hunted right at this moment. The thought of them fucking made her want to throw up.

With the help of a boost from Lester, Tyler got the loft-hatch open. As he pulled it down, a ladder extended, nearly colliding with his head. They signalled for Kerry to join them and then made their way up. Lester was the last one up, pulling up the ladder and closing the hatch behind him.

XXV

"Why is there evil in the world? Because sometimes you just wanna fuckin have it, and you don't care who gets hurt."

Joe Hill

25

Albert Parker rolled off his wife. A wicked grin plastered across his face. "We should let these little fuckers kill us more often."

"I don't know about that," she replied. "I feel rough."

He turned his attention towards Teri who was still conscious, but only just. "You need to feed," he said, gesturing towards the girl with the torn face.

Evelyn sat up and looked over at her supper. "Ah, my post coital cigarette," she laughed.

Whatever was about to happen to her, Teri hoped it was fast. She was in immense pain and her vanity was such that she wasn't sure she even wanted to make it out alive just to be considered a freak for the rest of her days. That didn't mean she wasn't scared though. She was terrified.

The naked old witch got to her feet and made her way towards the quivering, bloody mess that was Teri. As Evelyn sank down into a seated position in front her, Teri tried to protest, but no actual words were formed because her mouth was now entirely useless.

"Look at me honey," the old lady insisted. "It's easier if you don't try to fight."

Teri locked eyes with Evelyn for what was only intended to be a fleeting moment, but was suddenly powerless to look away. She felt like a battery being drained of its charge. There was nothing she could do except stare back and she suddenly felt exhausted. At least the pain in her face seemed to be ebbing away.

"Not too much, Love," Albert insisted. "Otherwise she is going to die pleasantly and you won't be able to kill her."

"Fine," she replied. She was feeling much better now. Energised and ready for some fun. She broke off her stare with Teri who slumped over, only semi-conscious now.

"Oh, no you don't," the old lady shouted. " I want you awake for this." She shuffled over and cradled Teri in her arms, pressing her head against her naked, wrinkled breasts. "Fetch me a knife, Albert," she barked at her husband. "I'm going to make this bitch even prettier."

Albert obliged and went to get her a knife. He returned, and handed it over, eager to see what his wife had in store for the snivelling little shit that was bleeding all over his carpet.

"I think, first of all I'm going to get rid of some of this loose skin." She pulled on a flap of what used to be lip and began sawing through the meat. Teri immediately began to scream. As the knife removed the first chunk of face, Evelyn threw it aside before pulling on another piece and repeating.

Teri was thrashing around wildly, trying to struggle free but she was no match for the sheer strength of the recently revitalized old woman. Piece by piece she removed more and more flesh until, throwing aside the final chunk of Teri's mouth, she raised her hands in the air triumphantly. "Ta-da," she hollered.

The old man came and stood next to his wife, inspecting her handiwork. "I think that might just be your masterpiece," he praised.

Teri's eyes rolled around in her head. She wanted to pass out. She was close to passing out. The only thing keeping her awake was the pain. There was no flesh around her mouth anymore. Her teeth and parts of her jaw were completely exposed. The once beautiful young woman was now a hideously deformed monster.

"I'm bored of her now," Evelyn said. She forced both of her hands into Teri's mouth, prizing her jaws apart. She leaned in and kissed Teri on the forehead and then in one swift motion, she tore Teri's lower jaw clean off. Teri's final moment on Earth were spent in an uncontrollable spasm, her death rattle, a gurgling, spluttering symphony as she drowned in her own blood.

Evelyn held Teri's jawbone up to her husband as if presenting a trophy. "Give me a kiss," she joked, as if the jaw was doing the talking.

XXVI

"He who searches for evil, must first look at his own reflection."

Confucious

26

They had barricaded themselves in the loft. The boys had found a heavy old chest and dragged it over the hatch, so that even if the old couple thought to look up there and tried to open the hatch, hopefully, the weight of the chest would keep them out that little bit longer.

Kerry was frantically searching for something she could weaponise herself with.

Tyler had devised a plan to see if he could break through the roof. Having looked around for something he could do some damage with, he found a loose brick that he liberated from its place in the wall, and with all the strength left in him, he began slamming it against the loft ceiling. Pieces of plasterboard began to crumble and break off with each swing of the brick.

The progress that Tyler was making inspired the others to locate something that they could use to assist him. Kerry found a length of two-by-four and quickly started swinging it at the boards. Lester, having found nothing of any use, started to pull pieces of the board away with his hands.

It wasn't long before they had broken enough plasterboard to expose the insulation. Tyler grabbed handfuls and started dragging it out of the cavity they had created. His hands instantly started to itch as its fibres imbedded in his skin. He ignored it and continued to clear it away, throwing large chunks of fibreglass to one side until he had a shot out the outer boards.

"We get through this and break the tiles off and we should be able to get out," he said, his voice full of excitement.

Lester wasn't so enthusiastic. "How do we get down once we're out?" he asked.

Tyler shrugged. "I don't know. I will worry about that once we're out of here."

Ignoring them both, Kerry continued attacking the roof. The outer panels were made of plywood and took a lot more to break through than the plasterboard had.

As she went in for another swing, the sound of the loft hatch opening broke her rhythm. She spun around, bringing the length of wood up in a defensive pose.

"Oh shit, they're here," Lester shouted.

Albert was the first one up the ladder to the chest that blocked his path. "Little pigs, little pigs, let me in," he taunted.

His wife snapped at him from the foot of the ladder. "Stop fucking around and just get up there."

Turning to look at her, he shook his head. "Can't a man have any fun?" he asked. He placed a hand on the bottom of the chest that had taken two grown men to drag and, with a slight heave, threw it clear of the hatch. It impacted against one of the wooden support beams, snapping it in half.

With clear access to his prey, he ascended the rest of the ladder and came face to face with the three remaining burglars. "Well, you three have certainly made for an interesting evening," he addressed them.

Without warning, Tyler snatched the length of wood from Kerry's hands and shoved her aside. He darted towards the old man, swinging the wood high above his head, determined to finish him off for good.

As it came thundering down towards his head, Albert caught hold of the timber with one hand while his other hand shot out, catching Tyler by the throat. With incredible speed and strength, Albert disarmed him and hoisted him off of his feet, holding him suspended in mid-air.

Evelyn appeared behind her husband in time to see the other two rush at him in a bid to free Tyler from his grip. With catlike agility, old lady Parker sprang into action. She leapt into the air and landed on Kerry, knocking her clean off her feet. As they crashed to the floor, Evelyn straddled Kerry. She sat across her torso, pinning her arms to the floor so that Kerry was utterly helpless.

Having armed himself with the brick that Tyler had been using to break through the roof, Lester swung it with all his might. It connected with the side of Albert's face, instantly breaking and relocating his jaw. The old man let go of Tyler who, being unprepared for the sudden drop, landed to the sound of a nauseating snap. He tumbled to the floor, his leg broken a piece of bone protruding through the flesh just above the ankle. Overwhelmed by the agony, Tyler yelled out as he clutched at his busted leg.

The old man lurched back from the blow that Lester had delivered him. He grasped at his face and with tears of pain filling his eyes he yanked at his jaw, snapping it back into place. "You dead little prick," he shouted, as he approached Lester, who was backing away as fast as he could. Menace was all he saw on the old man's face and suddenly he could back away no further. He hit the wall and was pinned.

"Nowhere to go you little fucker," he said, extending his old, prune-like hand towards Lester.

Evelyn placed her hand on Kerry's head, forcing it to turn in the direction of her husband and Kerry's boyfriend. "I want you to watch this," she said with a cackle.

Albert grabbed Lester by the shirt, shoving him hard against the wall. He leaned in towards Lester, his rancid breath filling Lester's nostrils. "Say goodbye to your girlfriend, maggot," he sneered.

Kerry looked on helplessly as the old man tore at the front of Lester's t-shirt. Lester began to scream as Albert Parker shoved his hand into his stomach, tearing at the skin as he worked his hand inside Lester's abdomen. With his gut breached, the old man took a handful of Lester's intestines. He pulled them out and lifted them to Lester's face. With a grin, he proudly flaunted them in front of his eyes. The last thing Lester heard as he slipped away was Kerry screaming.

XXVII

"Darkness dwells within even the best of us. In the worst of us, darkness not only dwells but reins."

Dean Koontz - Strange Highways

27

Having finally managed to get their two remaining guests out of the loft, the Parker's sat them on the same wooden chairs that they themselves had been tied to earlier that night.

Albert got on his knees and inspected the damage to Tyler's leg. "That looks like it hurts," he said with mock sympathy. He started flicking at the bone that poked out through the skin. Tyler roared with pain. "Yep, that definitely looks like it hurts," Albert laughed.

His wife pulled up a chair in front of the prisoners. "Will you stop fucking around and come sit down Albert," she scolded him.

Begrudgingly, he did as he was told and took a seat next to his wife.

"I imagine you both have lots of questions," The old lady said. Her eyes flicked across her captives who were not paying her the attention she demanded. "Hey!" She yelled at them both. "Look at me when I'm fucking talking to you." They both looked at the old lady through blurred, puffy eyes.

"That's better," she said with a smile. "Now, what would you like to know?"

It was Tyler who spoke first. His complexion now ghostly white. "Fuck you."

"Such a potty mouth," Evelyn replied. "Maybe I should get my husband to come and do something with that tongue of yours."

Tyler managed a slight, unenthusiastic laugh. "Tell that pussy to come do his worst." The sweat cascaded down Tyler's face. He was in bad shape, and he knew he didn't have any fight left in him, but he remained as defiant and feisty as ever.

A malevolent grin washed over the old lady's face. "I will overlook the fact that you're being such a foul-mouthed little fucker, as you don't have long left. Enjoy it while you can."

Taking hold of his wife's hand, it was Albert who spoke next. "Ok, so a little about what you have stumbled into tonight," he said. "We are what you might refer to as the spiders, and you sad pair of cunts are the flies."

"Basically, what he is trying to say," Evelyn added, "Is that you two dumb shits couldn't have picked a worse place to break into."

Kerry had had enough of the cryptic bullshit that she had been hearing all night and wanted an explanation. They had just killed the only person who had ever really loved her. What made it worse was that she had spent their time together treating him like dirt. It wasn't that she didn't love him back. It wasn't even that she wanted to treat him badly. She had spent her entire life being pushed from pillar to post by people that didn't really care for her and having found someone who truly seemed to care about her; she had no idea how to handle it.

Inevitably, they were going to die tonight and Kerry wasn't even afraid of that fact anymore. She had nothing left in the world. Maybe dying was the release that she desperately needed. "Are you going to get to the point or bore me to death because I'm sick of this shit," she hissed at the old couple.

"See, this is why I like this girl," Albert said, squeezing his wife's hand. "It almost breaks my heart that we have to kill her."

Evelyn patted her husband on the knee and smiled. "Maybe. We will see how it goes."

She turned back to guests. "So, questions?"

XXVIII

"The world needs more anger. The world often continues to allow evil because it isn't angry enough."

Bede Jarrett

28

Everything Kerry had just heard seemed ridiculous. While she had no way of explaining what she had witnessed tonight, she refused to accept that this wrinkled, disgusting pair of psychopaths were really, ancient demons.

The old couple had gone on to explain how there were many gateways to a realm that people often referred to as Hell, and this was just one such place. They claimed that they had been charged with guarding this gateway since man had first appeared on earth and that while they could do as they pleased to anyone foolish enough to trespass on their soil; they had to leave the outside world alone.

"You expect us to believe this bullshit?" Tyler had asked. "So, you're demons and this is Hell?"

"No, not quite," Albert corrected. "Were you not paying attention?"

"Evelyn butted in. "This is a gate to what you might call Hell. For you, I'm sure it will truly be Hellish. I guess you're going to find out soon enough."

With that, Albert got up out of his chair. "I need a cuppa tea," he said. "Who wants one?"

Evelyn shook her head and their hostages didn't respond so Albert made his way to the kitchen. "Suit yourselves."

As she watched him go, something struck Kerry as funny and she began to laugh, loud and obnoxious.

"What's so funny?" Evelyn asked, a little irritated.

Composing herself, Kerry answered her question with a question. "So ancient demons drink tea?"

The old lady had to admit, it did seem ludicrous and she found herself laughing at how preposterous it must have appeared. "We don't have to drink anything," she answered. " He just seems to like it. We only have to feed when we've been hurt or killed and you found out earlier how that works. We still eat, but only because we like it. Not because we must."

She remembered back to how Mr Parker had slowly drained her energy. It had been like having her very essence syphoned. Not an unpleasant experience, but one she didn't care to repeat.

"I think sometimes that the silly old bastard thinks he's human," the old lady continued.

The old man shuffled back into the living room. Kerry thought it funny how they moved like old people, but when it became necessary, they could move like cheetahs. 'Maybe it's all part of an act they have been putting on for so long that it's just become second nature,' she thought.

In one hand, Albert carried a mug of freshly made tea, which he set down next to his chair. In the other hand, he held a pan of what appeared to be boiling water. The steam that billowed from the pan gave it away.

Having discarded his beverage, Albert walked casually to where Tyler sat, bound to his chair and without saying a word, he emptied the contents of the pan over Tyler's head.

What took her by surprise the most was how Tyler didn't react straight away. It was like there was a delay between the boiling water drenching his head and his brain processing what had happened. Kerry thought that it could be the shock that caused him to not immediately register the severity of the situation. Once the pain penetrated his grey matter, Tyler began to howl at an inhuman pitch.

Unable to bring his hands up to his scalded face, Tyler writhed around in his chair with his head thrown back. The skin on his face bubbled and blistered and he kept his eyes clamped shut due to the pain where the water had instantly burned them. Had he been able to open them, his vision would have certainly been impaired, if not gone completely.

Kerry screamed at the old man for his actions. "You sick fucking bastard," she yelled. "You sick fuck!"

Albert Parker turned to Kerry and looked her over before replying. "Don't be such a hypocrite," he said. "You hate him. I could read it on you the moment I laid eyes on you. What do you care?"

"What?" Kerry asked, dumbfounded that he would think her feelings towards Tyler meant that she would think this was ok.

Albert laughed at her response. "He is a violent bully and a thug that has brought misery to virtually everyone he ever met. He had it coming."

Old lady Parker got out of her chair and wandered over to where Tyler sat. The steam that had poured from his face moments ago had finally subsided and while he had stopped screaming, for the time being, he now wept uncontrollably. His skin was raw and broken and resembled a vicious case of psoriasis and new blisters appeared constantly.

She examined him closely and while Tyler couldn't see her, he knew she was close. He could smell her breath. It smelt like damp mould. In one last act of defiance, Tyler delivered a well-placed headbutt. His forehead slammed into Evelyn's nose, breaking it instantly and delivering enough force to knock her off of her feet. She toppled backwards, hitting the back of her head on the floor as she crashed down onto the carpet.

She held her bent nose. Blood filled into a pool in her hand and dripped down onto her blue, floral dress. "That's the second time tonight one of you fuckers has broken my nose," she shrieked.

She gripped her nose between her fingers and with a loud crack, snapped it back into place. "Shit, that hurt."

Despite the pain that consumed his every thought and action, Tyler found it in him to laugh mockingly at the woman whom he had just assaulted. "Fucking Witch," he managed.

The old lady leapt to her feet. "I'll show you a fucking Witch," she hissed. She grabbed hold of Tyler's hair, yanking his head back. She leaned in and flicked her tongue along the length of his face. "Good night pretty boy," she whispered before using the long, sharp nail on her index finger to open his jugular. The blood that hit her dress this time was his. It squirted like a jet from the deep wound she had inflicted, spraying everything in a five-foot radius.

It was too much for Kerry who threw her head to one side and vomited violently.

Albert buried his head in his hands, frustrated. "This carpet is fucking ruined," he muttered.

XXIX

"The monstrous act by definition demands a monster."

Rick Yancey

29

For reasons that Kerry didn't quite understand, the old woman had spent considerable time cleaning her up. Since the boys had died, and she was the only one left, the Parkers instantly seemed to act much more pleasantly towards her. This change of attitude seemed baffling. She was certain they still intended to kill her. They were just being incredibly nice about it.

Albert Parker had even convinced her to have that cup of tea. She was more than a little relieved when he returned and she noticed he didn't have another pan of boiling water with him. She had accepted death. She hadn't factored a facial scalding into the bargain.

She no longer had any idea what time it was, but the sun had risen, so she figured it to be around 7ish. All her friends were dead. 'Friends?' she thought. 'Maybe that's a bit liberal.' Lester was gone though, and she had really cared for him. Even Tyler had become more dependable as the night drew on, though it was his fault they had ended up in this situation in the first place. She thought that over too. 'Was it really his fault? At no point had he held a gun to our heads.

We followed because we too were drawn in by the lure of easy money.'

They hadn't found any money and they had died for it anyway. Kerry had learned a lot this night. She now knew that demons were a thing. She had also learned that human or not, old people did not smell good up close and she realised what she had suspected all along. That she was ok with dying. The last realisation made her smile. Maybe if there were demons and a hell, then surely there had to be a heaven. 'Maybe I will see my sister again?' she wondered. That thought made her smile even more.

Evelyn noticed the smile on her face and knew what she was thinking. "The answer is no," she said, interrupting Kerry's thoughts.

Kerry gave her a quizzical look. "What?"

"You're wondering if there is a heaven. The answer is no. You see, you mortals think that if you're good people, you'll be rewarded with an eternity in some tranquil heaven full of harps and angels. What you don't seem to understand is that death is your reward."

Kerry didn't respond. She was baffled by the old lady's response and more so because she was responding to her unspoken thoughts.

Evelyn continued. "When you're truly bad people, one way or another, you pass through somewhere like here on a path to where you are going to spend an eternity of torment. This much is true. For good people, the reward is simply being able to die. There is no heaven. Only rest. You won't meet God or Gods. You won't spend forever in the arms of a lover. You just go."

"She's right you know," Albert piped up. That's as good as it gets."

"You came in here of your own free will," Evelyn added. That usually never happens. Your destination would have been the same but your choice to come here of your own free will is mind-blowing."

"Oh, but don't worry though," Albert interrupted once again. "You might very well see your sister again."

Kerry looked disgusted and sickened by his last comment. "Why would she be in hell? She was just a kid."

Albert laughed at her suggestion that her age would play any part in keeping her from eternal torment. "You really should have attended Sunday school young lady. Your sister committed a sin. Thou shalt not kill. Not even yourself."

"She had been raped. She didn't know what she was doing." The tears streamed down Kerry's cheeks. Her voice raised through anger and hurt. "Why would God punish a kid for that?"

"As I have already explained child, I don't even know that there is a God. There are just rules. Rules that me and Evelyn here are put here to enforce."

"I know it doesn't seem fair, child," Evelyn added. "Life isn't always fair, and neither, it would seem, is the afterlife. Still, planning to relieve an old couple of their worldly possessions isn't exactly fair either, so it's swings and roundabouts really."

Albert nodded in agreement. "You reap what you sow honey."

XXX

"The greater evil who is in-
When both in wayward paths are straying?
The poor sinner for the pain
Or he who pays for the sin?"

Sor Juana Inés de la Cruz

30

Kerry had finished her tea. She was surprised how much she had enjoyed it given her circumstances. At least it had helped wash away the taste of sick. She felt calm for someone who had watched her friends die. For someone who knew that their time was almost certainly at an end.

She had frequently considered ending her life. She wasn't a religious person, but she had figured that if there was even the slightest chance she would get to see her sister again, then it could be worth the risk. Plus, now she had nobody left. She was truly alone. So what did it matter if she died? Why should she care?

Evelyn Parker was very aware of her feelings. "I told you earlier, there is every chance you will see your sister again," she said, interrupting Kerry's thoughts.

Kerry looked up at the old lady. She couldn't hide her confusion over the old woman's words. "What?"

"Your thoughts had drifted to seeing your sister in the afterlife," she replied. "You should be careful what you wish for."

Kerry remembered the comments the couple had made earlier about suicide being a mortal sin and how her sister would have to pay for eternity. She had figured they were just being cruel.

"No ill deed goes unpunished," Albert interjected. "Your entire, miserable life has been a series of ill deeds. I was genuinely growing to like you, but it is what it is."

Evelyn couldn't help but laugh at her husband's last comment. "I'm convinced he's going soft in his old age." The laughter stopped as abruptly as it had started and her face became more business-like. "I can read your thoughts dear. That's what you were wondering. How I know what you're feeling."

Kerry had heard it all. Defiantly she looked the old lady in the eye. "Fine, what am I thinking now then?" she challenged.

This seemed to piss the old Witch off. She smacked Kerry around the ear before walking back to her chair. "Do I look like I'm here to perform parlour tricks for your amusement?" She barked. "I've been here for thousands of years. I don't jump through hoops to entertain you rotting flesh sacks, so show some fucking respect."

That she had managed to get under the woman's skin brought a smile to Kerry's face. She didn't have much to smile about so she would take it where she could find it.

"The fact of the matter is, we knew you were coming before you ever got here," Albert continued, ignoring his wife's outburst.

"If that were true, then why were you in bed? Why did you leave us to ransack the place? Why wait until Tyler came and dragged you out of bed? We could have given up and left before any of that happened, so then what?"

Evelyn laughed at the suggestion that they hadn't been in complete control the whole time. "You think that once you entered this house that you had free will to just leave? You're more naïve then I thought."

Once again her husband interrupted. "We saw you on those night's that you sat outside in that van, eyeing up our property. We knew you were there. We could hear you."

"That's right," Evelyn continued. "We weren't sure exactly what night to expect you, but we knew you would be coming and the minute you entered this house you were ours. You were never leaving if we didn't wish it.

"It's been so many years since we have had this much fun," Albert added.

None of this made much sense to Kerry. "So, why didn't you just kill us the minute we walked in?" she asked.

"And spoil all that fun?" the old lady scoffed. "It was far more interesting to let you think you had the upper hand for a while. It made the old switcharoo much more exciting."

"We might be old as shit, as I'm sure your boyfriend put it, but we still deserve a little fun," Albert said. "You were fucked from the minute you decided to turn this place over."

The old lady got out of her chair and once again, walked over to the chair-bound captive. "So, now it's down to us to decide how best to punish you. We always get off on this bit."

Old lady Parker placed her hands on either side of Kerry's head and closed her eyes. "Let's dig nice and deep and see what really makes your skin crawl."

Kerry's head felt like it had been filled with a colony of angry bees. They swarmed in her brain, vibrating their wings and stinging her grey matter. She held on for as long as she could while the old woman mind-raped her. Until it all became too much: Kerry blanked out.

XXXI

"Those who grant sympathy to guilt, grant none to innocence."

Ayn Rand

31

Mr and Mrs Parker climbed back into bed. Albert Parker had made himself another of his beloved cups of tea. 'These humans are definitely on to something here,' he thought to himself, regarding is steaming, milky, brown brew.

His wife had grabbed the book she was currently reading. A few chapters of Death on the Nile should help her drift off.

The sun was up now and the birds had finished their dawn choir practice, but it had been a busy night and the Parker's were not as young as they used to be. "A few centuries past their prime," Albert Parker had joked.

Disposing of all the bodies had been easy enough. The Parkers owned a walk-in freezer that occupied the basement under the house. Access to the basement came by a hatch that lay hidden under the living room carpet. Evelyn and Albert had dragged the corpses of the failed burglars down the steps and pinned them on meat hooks suspended from the freezer ceiling. They figured that they would make good eating, come the colder winter months. Especially the one they had called Shane. There was plenty of meat on him.

As he lay in bed enjoying his brew, Albert couldn't help but mull over the events of the night. "Do you think this has happened to any of the others?" he asked.

His wife looked up from her book, visibly irked that he had interrupted her reading. "I hope so for their sake," she said with a grin. "You really liked the blonde one, didn't you?"

"Yeah, there was something about her that the others didn't have," he answered.

"I know exactly what it was," Evelyn replied. "She was tortured before we ever got our hands on her."

Albert thought it over for a moment. "Yes, that's true, but it was something else. She didn't belong with the rest of them. It almost seems a shame we couldn't have kept her."

His wife laughed at the suggestion. "She isn't a stray puppy," she mocked. "You want we should put a collar on her and teach her to shit in the garden?"

Albert finished his tea and covered himself over with the quilt, annoyed by his wife's jibes. "That isn't what I meant."

Don't get huffy, I know what you meant. What's done is done. She is exactly where she deserves to be and that's all there is to it."

The old man didn't reply. He closed his eyes, having felt that he had earned some rest.

Evelyn turned back to her book. 'Now where was I?' she thought.

XXXII

"The season of evil," I echoed. "Protect your soul."

David Almond

32

Kerry Jones found herself suffocated by the darkness that enveloped her. She saw nothing but black. Her other senses were working overtime though. That putrid aroma. It filled her nasal cavity and reminded her of the smell from a butcher's shop, only all the meat would have had to have gone rancid first. It made her stomach perform somersaults. A constant feeling of needing to vomit, yet the sickness never came.

Then the screaming started. High-pitched, shrill shrieks. She felt like her ears might explode as the screams caused her eardrums to vibrate painfully.

She clamped her hands over her ears but it didn't help. The sound just grew louder.

Suddenly, she didn't feel quite so alone. She couldn't see them, but she knew they were there. Surrounding her, moving closer and closer. Who was it? As the unseen visitors flanked, Kerry became overwhelmed with a claustrophobic panic.

The screams grew louder the closer, whatever-they-were, came near her. Yet, while they seemed almost on top of her, nothing touched her.

'It's just a dream she thought,' trying to calm herself down.' She tried breathing deep to slow her heart rate. 'It's my nightmare. I will wake up soon enough.' She continued to breathe. It did nothing to help with the pungent smell of death and decay that turned her stomach.

Her ears suddenly picked another sound from among the screams. This one was different. This was words. They were drowned out at first by the shrieking, but as she listened more intently, she began to make out what those words were. A voice crying out to be helped. A woman's voice, clearly very distressed. It grew louder the more she listened for it.

"Please, God, help me!" the voice called out, pleading, and suddenly Kerry recognised who it belonged to. It was her sister, Abbie. She sounded hurt. She sounded scared. She sounded like she was dying.

Kerry could no longer control her breathing. Her heart began to race once again, and the panic doubled.

"Please let me wake up," she said to herself. "Please let me wake up."

Usually, by now she would spring up in her bed, doused in sweat and disoriented.

"Please let me wake up, she begged. Her begging turned to a loud, shrill pleading that blended in with the chorus of cries from the other voices, lost in the darkness. "Why can't I fucking wake up?.."

The end

ABOUT THE AUTHOR

Lee Richmond was born in the swampy marshlands of East Anglia. Fed on a steady diet of fast, snotty punk rock and 80s slasher movies, it was only a matter of time before the sick, twisted imagery that festered in his head eventually found its way to the page.

Lee was influenced from a very early age by the films of John Carpenter, Dario Argento, Wes Craven and Tobe Hooper and the books of Clive Barker, Stephen King and James Herbert.

Music also plays its part in influencing Lee's writing. His love for bands like The Misfits, Ramones, Fugazi and Sisters of Mercy and the works of such movie composers as Hans Zimmer and Christopher Young.

Lee's other interests include playing bass guitar and drawing. He also owns and writes for horror movie website, reelhorrorshow.co.uk along with fellow writer, Mark Green.

MORE FROM THIS AUTHOR

Made in the USA
Columbia, SC
15 October 2023

24461899R00102